The Rupa Book of Ruskin Bond's
Himalayan Tales

Ruskin Bond has been writing for over sixty years, and has now over 120 titles in print—novels, collection of short stories, poetry, essays, anthologies and books for children. His first novel, *The Room on the Roof*, received the prestigious John Llewellyn Rhys Award in 1957. He has also received the Padma Shri (1999), the Padma Bhushan (2014) and two awards from Sahitya Akademi—one for his short stories and another for his writings for children. In 2012, the Delhi government gave him its Lifetime Achievement Award.

Born in 1934, Ruskin Bond grew up in Jamnagar, Shimla, New Delhi and Dehradun. Apart from three years in UK, he has spent all his life in India, and now lives in Mussoorie with his adopted family.

By the same author

A Little Book of Friendship
A Little Book of Life
A Little Night Music
A Long Walk for Bina (Illustrated)
A Song of Many Rivers
All Roads Lead to Ganga
Angry River (Illustrated)
Falling in Love Again
Funny Side Up
Ghost Stories From the Raj
Great Stories for Children
Hanuman to the Rescue (Illustrated)
Monkey Trouble and Other Grandfather Stories
My Favourite Nature Stories
No Man Is An Island
Once Upon A Time in the Doon
Party Time in Mussoorie
Potpourri
Roads to Mussoorie
Romi and the Wildfire (Illustrated)
Ruskin Bond's Children's Omnibus
School Days
School Times
Stories Short and Sweet (Illustrated)
Strange Men Strange Places
Tales and Legends From India
The Beast Tamer
The Big Book of Animal Stories
The Blue Umbrella (Illustrated)
The Children's Companion
The Empty House
The Essential Collection for Young Readers
The India I Love
The Jungle Omnibus
The Lagoon
The Laughing Skull
The Perfect Murder
The Prospects of Flowers
The Road to the Bazaar
The Rupa Book of Great Suspense Stories
The Rupa Book of Haunted Houses
The Rupa Book of Heartwarming Stories
The Rupa Book of Scary Stories
The Rupa Book of Shikar Stories
The Rupa Book of Snappy Surprises
The Rupa Book of Travellers' Tales
The Rupa Book of Wicked Stories
The Rupa Laughter Omnibus
The Ruskin Bond Horror Omnibus
The Ruskin Bond Mini Bus
The Very Best of Ruskin Bond
The Whistling Schoolboy and Other Stories of School Life
The White Tiger and Other Stories
The World Outside My Window
Tigers for Dinner
Too Much Trouble
Voting at Fosterganj
White Clouds, Green Mountains
Who Kissed Me in the Dark

The Rupa Book of Ruskin Bond's
Himalayan Tales

Published by
Rupa Publications India Pvt. Ltd 2013
7/16, Ansari Road, Daryaganj
New Delhi 110002

Sales centres:
Allahabad Bengaluru Chennai
Hyderabad Jaipur Kathmandu
Kolkata Mumbai

Copyright © Ruskin Bond 2003, 2013

This is a work of fiction. Names, characters, places and incidents
are either the product of the author's imagination or are used fictitiously
and any resemblance to any actual person, living or dead, events or
locales is entirely coincidental.

All rights reserved.
No part of this publication may be reproduced, transmitted,
or stored in a retrieval system, in any form or by any means,
electronic, mechanical, photocopying, recording or otherwise,
without the prior permission of the publisher.

ISBN: 978-81-291-0144-0

Twenty-first impression 2023

25 24 23 22 21

The moral right of the author has been asserted.

Printed in India

This book is sold subject to the condition that it shall not, by way
of trade or otherwise, be lent, resold, hired out, or otherwise circulated,
without the publisher's prior consent, in any form of binding or cover
other than that in which it is published.

Sweet Dolly

Sweet Dolly, you're the girl for me,
Kind Dolly, I shall always see
You climbing in your father's garden,
Picking apples off a tree,
Sorting out the rosy ones,
And giving them to me

Contents

On Wings of Sleep	1
The Wind on Haunted Hill	3
Mother Hill	10
The Whistling Schoolboy	13
Song of the Whistling Thrush	14
The Night the Roof Blew Off	19
The Cherry Tree	24
From the Pool to the Glacier	32
The Last Truck Ride	60
A Walk through Garhwal	69
Haikus and Other Short Verses	81
A Long Walk for Bina	84
These Simple Things	112
Mussoorie's Landour Bazaar	114

The Old Lama 122
Visitors from the Forest 126
A Bouquet of Love 130

On Wings of Sleep

On wings of sleep
I dreamt I flew
Across the valley drenched in dew
Over the roof-tops
Into the forest
Swooping low
Where the Sambhur belled
And the peacocks flew.
And the dawn broke
Rose-pink behind the mountains
And the river ran silver and gold
As I glided over the trees
Drifting with the dawn breeze
Across the river,
over fields of corn.

And the world awoke
To a new day, a new dawn.

Time to fly home,
As the sun rose, red and angry,
Ready to singe my wings,
I returned to my sleeping form,
Creaking bed and dusty window-pane,
To dream of flying with the wind again.

The Wind on Haunted Hill

Whoo, whoo, whoo, cried the wind as it swept down from the Himalayan snows. It hurried over the hills and passes and hummed and moaned through the tall pines and deodars. There was little on Haunted Hill to stop the wind—only a few stunted trees and bushes and the ruins of a small settlement.

On the slopes of the next hill was a village. People kept large stones on their tin roofs to prevent them from being blown off. There was nearly always a strong wind in these parts. Three children were spreading clothes out to dry on a low stone wall, putting a stone on each piece.

Eleven-year-old Usha, dark-haired and rose-cheeked, struggled with her grandfather's long, loose shirt. Her younger brother, Suresh, was doing his best to hold down a bedsheet, while Usha's friend, Binya, a slightly older girl, helped.

Once everything was firmly held down by stones, they climbed up on the flat rocks and sat there sunbathing and staring across the fields at the ruins on Haunted Hill.

"I must go to the bazaar today," said Usha.

"I wish I could come too," said Binya. "But I have to help with the cows."

"I can come!" said eight-year-old Suresh. He was always ready to visit the bazaar, which was three miles away, on the other side of the hill.

"No, you can't," said Usha. "You must help Grandfather chop wood."

"Won't you feel scared returning alone?" he asked. "There are ghosts on Haunted Hill!"

"I'll be back before dark. Ghosts don't appear during the day."

"Are there lots of ghosts in the ruins?" asked Binya.

"Grandfather says so. He says that over a hundred years ago, some Britishers lived on the hill. But the settlement was always being struck by lightning, so they moved away."

"But if they left, why is the place visited by ghosts?"

"Because—Grandfather says—during a terrible storm, one of the houses was hit by lightning, and everyone in it was killed. Even the children."

"How many children?"

"Two. A boy and his sister. Grandfather saw them playing there in the moonlight."

"Wasn't he frightened?"

"No. Old people don't mind ghosts."

Usha set out for the bazaar at two in the afternoon. It was about an hour's walk. The path went through yellow fields of flowering mustard, then along the saddle of the hill, and up, straight through the ruins. Usha had often gone that way to shop at the bazaar or to see her aunt, who lived in the town nearby.

Wild flowers bloomed on the crumbling walls of the ruins, and a wild plum tree grew straight out of the floor of what had once been a hall. It was covered with soft, white blossoms. Lizards scuttled over the stones, while a whistling thrush, its deep purple plumage glistening in the sunshine, sat on a window-sill and sang its heart out.

Usha sang too, as she skipped lightly along the path, which dipped steeply down to the valley and led to the little town with its quaint bazaar.

Moving leisurely, Usha bought spices, sugar and matches. With the two rupees she had saved from her pocket-money, she chose a necklace of amber-coloured beads for herself and some marbles for Suresh. Then she had her mother's slippers repaired at a cobbler's shop.

Finally, Usha went to visit Aunt Lakshmi at her flat above the shops. They were talking and drinking cups of hot, sweet tea when Usha realized that dark clouds had gathered over the mountains. She quickly picked up her things, said good-bye to her aunt, and set out for the village.

Strangely, the wind had dropped. The trees were still, the crickets silent. The crows flew round in circles, then settled in an oak tree.

'I must get home before dark,' thought Usha, hurrying along the path.

But the sky had darkened and a deep rumble echoed over the hills. Usha felt the first heavy drop of rain hit her cheek. Holding the shopping bag close to her body, she quickened her pace until she was almost running. The raindrops were coming down faster now—cold, stinging pellets of rain. A flash of lightning sharply outlined the ruins on the hill, and then all was dark again. Night had fallen.

'I'll have to shelter in the ruins,' Usha thought and began to run. Suddenly the wind sprang up again, but she did not have to fight it. It was behind her now, helping her along, up the steep path and on to the brow of the hill. There was another flash of lightning, followed by a peal of thunder. The ruins loomed before her, grim and forbidding.

Usha remembered part of an old roof that would give some shelter. It would be better than trying to go on. In the dark, with the howling wind, she might stray off the path and fall over the edge of the cliff.

Whoo, whoo, whoo, howled the wind. Usha saw the wild plum tree swaying, its foliage thrashing against the ground. She found her way into the ruins, helped by the constant flicker of lightning. Usha placed her hands flat against a stone wall and moved sideways, hoping to reach the sheltered corner. Suddenly, her hand touched something soft and furry, and she gave a startled cry. Her cry was answered by another—half snarl, half screech—as something leapt away in the darkness.

With a sigh of relief Usha realized that it was the cat that lived in the ruins. For a moment she had been frightened, but now she moved quickly along the wall until she heard the rain drumming on a remnant of a tin roof. Crouched in a corner, she found some shelter. But the tin sheet groaned and clattered as if it would sail away any moment.

Usha remembered that across this empty room stood an old fireplace. Perhaps it would be drier there under the blocked chimney. But she would not attempt to find it just now—she might lose her way altogether.

Her clothes were soaked and water streamed down from her hair, forming a puddle at her feet. She thought she heard a faint cry—the cat again, or an owl? Then the storm blotted out all other sounds.

There had been no time to think of ghosts, but now that she was settled in one place, Usha remembered Grandfather's story about the lightning-blasted ruins. She hoped and prayed that lightning would not strike her.

Thunder boomed over the hills, and the lightning came quicker now. Then there was a bigger flash, and for a moment the entire ruin was lit up. A streak of blue sizzled along the floor of the building. Usha was staring straight ahead, and, as the opposite wall lit up, she saw, crouching in front of the unused fireplace, two small figures—children!

The ghostly figures seemed to look up and stare back at Usha. And then everything was dark again.

Usha's heart was in her mouth. She had seen without doubt, two ghosts on the other side of the room. She wasn't going to remain in the ruins one minute longer.

She ran towards the big gap in the wall through which she had entered. She was halfway across the open space when something—someone—fell against her. Usha stumbled, got up, and again bumped into something. She gave a frightened scream. Someone else screamed. And then there was a shout, a boy's shout, and Usha instantly recognized the voice.

"Suresh!"

"Usha!"

"Binya!"

They fell into each other's arms, so surprised and relieved that all they could do was laugh and giggle and repeat each other's names.

Then Usha said, "I thought you were ghosts."

"We thought you were a ghost," said Suresh.

"Come back under the roof," said Usha.

They huddled together in the corner, chattering with excitement and relief.

"When it grew dark, we came looking for you," said Binya. "And then the storm broke."

"Shall we run back together?" asked Usha. "I don't want to stay here any longer."

"We'll have to wait," said Binya. "The path has fallen away at one place. It won't be safe in the dark, in all this rain."

"We'll have to wait till morning," said Suresh, "and I'm so hungry!"

The storm continued, but they were not afraid now. They gave each other warmth and confidence. Even the ruins did not seem so forbidding.

After an hour the rain stopped, and the thunder grew more distant.

Towards dawn the whistling thrush began to sing. Its sweet, broken notes flooded the ruins with music. As the sky grew lighter, they saw that the plum tree stood upright again, though it had lost all its blossoms.

"Let's go," said Usha.

Outside the ruins, walking along the brow of the hill, they watched the sky grow pink. When they were some distance away, Usha looked back and said, "Can you see something behind the wall? It's like a hand waving."

"It's just the top of the plum tree," said Binya.

"Good-bye, good-bye ..." They heard voices.

"Who said 'good-bye'?" asked Usha.

"Not I," said Suresh.

"Not I," said Binya.

"I heard someone calling," said Usha.

"It's only the wind," assured Binya.

Usha looked back at the ruins. The sun had come up and was touching the top of the wall.

"Come on," said Suresh. "I'm hungry."

They hurried along the path to the village.

"Good-bye, good-bye ..." Usha heard them calling. Was it just the wind?

Mother Hill

It is hard to realize that I've been here all these years—twenty-five summers, winters and Himalayan springs. When I look back to the time of my first coming here, it does seem like yesterday.

That probably sums it all up. Time passes, and yet it doesn't pass; people come and go, the mountains remain. Mountains are permanent things. They are stubborn, they refuse to move. You can blast holes out of them for their mineral wealth, strip them of their trees and foliage, or dam their streams and divert their currents. You can make tunnels and roads and bridges; but no matter how hard they try, humans cannot actually get rid of the mountains. That's what I like about them; they are here to stay.

I like to think that I have become a part of these mountains, this particular range, and that by living here for so long, I am able to claim a relationship with the trees, wild flowers, and even the rocks that are an integral part of it.

Yesterday at twilight, when I passed beneath a canopy of oak leaves, I felt that I was a part of the forest. I put out my hand and touched the bark of an old tree, and as I turned away, its leaves brushed against my face as if to acknowledge me.

One day, I thought, if we trouble these great creatures too much, and hack away at them and destroy their young, they will simply uproot themselves and march away, whole forests on the move, over the next range and next, far from the haunts of man. I have seen many forests and green places dwindle and disappear. Now there is an outcry. It is suddenly fashionable to be an environmentalist. That's all right. Perhaps, it is not too late to save the little that is left.

By and large, writers have to stay in the plains to make a living. Hill people have their work cut out trying to wrest a livelihood from their thin, calcinated soil. And as for mountaineers, they climb their peaks and move on in search of other peaks.

But to me, as a writer, mountains have been kind. They were kind from the beginning, when I left a job in Delhi and rented a small cottage on the outskirts of the hill-station. Today, most hill-stations are rich men's playgrounds, but years ago they were places where people of modest means would live quite cheaply. There were few cars and everyone walked about.

The cottage was on the edge of an oak and maple forest and I spent eight or nine years in it, most of them happy, writing stories, essays, poems and books for children. I think this had something to do with Prem's children. He and his wife had taken on the job of looking after the house and all practical matters (I remain helpless with fuses, clogged cisterns, leaking gas cylinders, ruptured water pipes, tin roofs that blow away when there is a storm, and the do-it-yourself world of small-town India).

Naturally, I grew attached to them and became a part of the family, an adopted grandfather. For Rakesh, I wrote a story about a cherry tree that had difficulty in growing up. For Mukesh, who liked upheavals, I wrote a story about an earthquake and put him in it, and for Dolly I wrote rhymes.

'Who goes to the Hills, goes to his Mother', wrote Kipling, and he seldom wrote truer words. For living in the hills was like living in the bosom of a strong, sometimes proud, but always a comforting mother. And every time I went away, the homecoming would be tender and precious. It became increasingly difficult for me to go away.

It has not always been happiness and light though. There were times when money ran out. Editorial doors sometimes close; but when one door closes another has, for me, almost immediately, miraculously opened.

When you have received love from people and the freedom that only mountains can give, then you have come very near the borders of Heaven.

The Whistling Schoolboy

From the gorge above Gangotri
Down to Kochi by the sea,
The whistling thrush keeps singing
That same sweet melody.

He was a whistling schoolboy once,
Who heard god Krishna's flute,
And tried to play the same sweet tune,
But touched a faulty note.

Said Krishna to the errant youth—
A bird you must become,
And you shall whistle all your days
Until your song is done.

Song of the Whistling Thrush

I had been in the hills for a few days when I heard the song of the Himalayan whistling thrush. I did not see the bird that day. It kept to the deep shadows of the ravine below the old stone cottage. I was sitting at the window, gazing out at the new leaves on the walnut and wild pear trees. All was still; the wind was at peace with itself, the mountains brooded massively under the darkening sky. Then, emerging from the depths of the forest like a dark, sweet secret, came the indescribably beautiful call of the whistling thrush.

It is a song that never fails to thrill me. The bird starts with a hesitant schoolboy whistle, as though trying out the melody; then, confident of the tune, it bursts into full song, a crescendo of sweet notes and variations that ring clearly across the hillside. Then suddenly the song breaks off, right in the middle of a cadenza, and the enchanted listener is left wondering what happened to the bird to make it stop so suddenly. Nothing, really, because a few moments later the song is taken up again.

At first the bird was heard but never seen. Then one day I found the whistling thrush perched on the garden fence. He was a deep, glistening purple, his shoulders flecked with white; he had sturdy black legs and a strong yellow beak; rather a dapper fellow, who could have looked well in a top hat dancing with Fred Astaire. When he saw me coming down the path he uttered a sharp kree-ee—unexpectedly harsh when one remembered his singing—and flew away into the shadowed ravine.

But as the months passed he grew used to my presence and became less shy. One of my rainwater pipes had blocked, resulting in an overflow and a small permanent puddle under the stone steps. This became the thrush's favourite bathing place. On sultry summer afternoons, while I was taking a siesta upstairs, I would hear the bird flapping about in the rainwater pool. A little later, refreshed and sunning himself on the tin roof, he would treat me to a little concert, performed, I cannot help feeling, especially for my benefit.

It was Prakash, the man who brought my milk, who told me the story of the whistling thrush, or the Kastura or Kaljit, as the hillmen called the bird. According to legend, the god Krishna fell asleep near a mountain stream, and while he slept, a small boy made off with his famous flute. On waking up and finding his flute gone, Krishna was so angry that he changed the culprit into a bird; but the boy had played on the flute and learned some of Krishna's wonderful music, and even as a bird he continued, in his disrespectful fashion, to whistle the music of the gods, only stopping now and then (as the whistling thrush does) when he couldn't remember the right tune.

It wasn't long before my thrush was joined by a female, who was exactly like him (in fact, I have never been able to tell one from the other). The pair did not sing duets, like Nelson Eddy and Jeanette MacDonald,* but preferred to give solo performances, waiting for each other to finish before bursting into song. When, as sometimes happened, they started off together, the effect was not so pleasing to my human ear.

These were love calls, no doubt, and it wasn't long before the pair were making forays into the rocky ledges of the ravine, looking for a suitable nesting site; but a couple of years were to pass before I saw any of their young.

After almost two years in the hills, I came to realise that these were birds "for all seasons". They were liveliest in midsummer, but even in the depths of winter, with snow lying on the ground, they would suddenly start singing as they flitted from pine to oak to naked chestnut.

As I write, there is a strong wind rushing through the trees and bustling in the chimney, while distant thunder threatens a summer storm. Undismayed, the whistling

---

* Famous singers from my boyhood.

thrushes are calling to each other as they roam the wind-threshed forest.

At other times I have heard them clearly above the sound of rushing water. And sometimes they leave the vicinity of the cottage and fly down to the stream, half a mile away, sending me little messages on the wind. Down there, they are busy snapping up snails and insects, the chief items on their menu.

Whistling thrushes usually nest on rocky ledges, near water, but my overtures of friendship may have given my visitors other ideas. Recently I was away from Mussoorie for about a fortnight. When I returned I was about to open the window when I noticed a large bundle of ferns, lichen, grass, mud and moss balanced outside on the window ledge. Peering through the glass, I was able to recognise this untidy basket as a nest. Could such tidy birds make such untidy nests? Indeed they could, because they arrived and proved their ownership a few minutes later.

Well, of course that meant I couldn't open the window any more—the nest would have gone over the ledge if I had. Fortunately, the room has another window and I kept this one open to let in sunshine, fresh air, and the music of birds, cicadas, and the ever welcome postman.

And now, this very day, three pink, freckled eggs lie in the cup of moss that forms the nursery in this jumble of a nest. The parent birds, both male and female, come and go, bustling about very efficiently, fully prepared for the great day that's coming about a fortnight hence.

One small thought occurs to me. The song of one thrush was bright and cheerful. The song of two thrushes was loud and joyful. But won't a choir of five whistling thrushes be a little too much for a solitary writer trying to concentrate at his typewriter? Will I have to make a choice between writing or listening to the birds? Will I have to hand the cottage to other denizens of the forest? Well, we shall have to wait and see. If readers do not hear from me again, they will know who to blame!

The Night the Roof Blew Off

We are used to sudden storms, up here on the first range of the Himalayas. The old building in which we live has, for more than a hundred years, received the full force of the wind as it sweeps across the hills from the east.

We'd lived in the building for more than ten years without a disaster. It had even taken the shock of a severe earthquake. As my granddaughter Dolly said, "It's difficult to tell the new cracks from the old!"

It's a two-storey building, and I live on the upper floor with my family: my three grandchildren and their parents. The roof is made of corrugated tin sheets, the ceiling of wooden boards. That's the traditional Mussoorie roof. (Mussoorie is a popular resort town perched on the side of a steep mountain in northern India.)

Looking back at the experience, it was the sort of thing that should have happened in a James Thurber story, like the dam that burst or the ghost who got in. But I wasn't thinking of Thurber at the time, although a few of his books were among the many I was trying to save from the icy rain pouring into my bedroom.

Our roof had held fast in many a storm, but the wind that night was really fierce. It came rushing at us with a high-pitched, eerie wail. The old roof groaned and protested. It took a battering for several hours while the rain lashed against the windows and the lights kept coming and going.

There was no question of sleeping, but we remained in bed for warmth and comfort. The fire had long since gone out, as the chimney had collapsed, bringing down a shower of sooty rainwater.

After about four hours of buffeting, the roof could take it no longer. My bedroom faces east, so my portion of the roof was the first to go.

The wind got under it and kept pushing until, with a ripping, groaning sound, the metal sheets shifted and slid off the rafters, some of them dropping with claps like thunder on to the road below.

So that's it, I thought. Nothing worse can happen. As long as the ceiling stays on, I'm not getting out of bed. We'll collect our roof in the morning.

Icy water splashing down on my face made me change my mind in a hurry. Leaping from the bed, I found that much of the ceiling had gone, too. Water was pouring on my open typewriter as well as on the bedside radio and bed cover.

Picking up my precious typewriter (my companion for thirty years) I stumbled into the front sitting room (and library), only to find a similar situation there. Water was pouring through the slats of the wooden ceiling, raining down on the open bookshelves.

By now I had been joined by the children, who had come to my rescue. Their section of the roof hadn't gone as yet. Their parents were struggling to close a window that had burst open, letting in lashings of wind and rain.

"Save the books!" shouted Dolly, the youngest, and that became our rallying cry for the next hour or two.

Dolly and her brother Mukesh picked up armfuls of books and carried them into their room. But the floor was awash, so the books had to be piled on their beds. Dolly was helping me gather some of my papers when a large field rat jumped on to the desk in front of her. Dolly squealed and ran for the door.

"It's all right," said Mukesh, whose love of animals extends even to field rats. "It's only sheltering from the storm."

Big brother Rakesh whistled for our dog, Tony, but Tony wasn't interested in rats just then. He had taken shelter in the kitchen, the only dry spot in the house.

Two rooms were now practically roofless, and we could see the sky lit up by flashes of lightning.

There were fireworks indoors, too, as water spluttered and crackled along a damaged wire. Then the lights went out altogether.

Rakesh, at his best in an emergency, had already lit two kerosene lamps. And by their light we continued to transfer books, papers, and clothes to the children's room.

We noticed that the water on the floor was beginning to subside a little.

"Where is it going?" asked Dolly.

"Through the floor," said Mukesh. "Down to the flat below!"

Cries of concern from our downstairs neighbours told us that they were having their share of the flood.

Our feet were freezing because there hadn't been time to put on proper footwear. And besides, shoes and slippers were awash by now. All chairs and tables were piled high with books. I hadn't realized the extent of my library until that night!

The available beds were pushed into the driest corner of the children's room, and there, huddled in blankets and quilts, we spent the remaining hours of the night while the storm continued.

Toward morning the wind fell, and it began to snow. Through the door to the sitting room I could see snowflakes drifting through the gaps in the ceiling, settling on picture-frames. Ordinary things like a glue bottle and a small clock took on a certain beauty when covered with soft snow.

Most of us dozed off.

When dawn came, we found the windowpanes encrusted with snow and icicles. The rising sun struck through the gaps in the ceiling and turned everything golden. Snow crystals glistened on the empty bookshelves. But the books had been saved.

Rakesh went out to find a carpenter and a tinsmith, while the rest of us started putting things in the sun to dry. By evening we'd put much of the roof back on.

It's a much-improved roof now, and we look forward to the next storm with confidence!

The Cherry Tree

One day, when Rakesh was six, he walked home from the Mussoorie bazaar eating cherries. They were a little sweet, a little sour; small, bright red cherries, which had come all the way from the Kashmir Valley.

Here in the Himalayan foothills where Rakesh lived, there were not many fruit trees. The soil was stony, and the dry cold winds stunted the growth of most plants. But on the more sheltered slopes there were forests of oak and deodar.

Rakesh lived with his grandfather on the outskirts of Mussoorie, just where the forest began. His father and mother lived in a small village fifty miles away, where they grew maize and rice and barley in narrow terraced fields on the lower slopes of the mountain. But there were no schools in the village, and Rakesh's parents were keen that he should go to school. As soon as he was of school-going age, they sent him to stay with his grandfather in Mussoorie. He had a little cottage outside the town.

Rakesh was on his way home from school when he bought the cherries. He paid fifty paise for the bunch. It took him about half-an-hour to walk home, and by the time he reached the cottage there were only three cherries left.

'Have a cherry, Grandfather,' he said, as soon as he saw his grandfather in the garden.

Grandfather took one cherry and Rakesh promptly ate the other two. He kept the last seed in this mouth for some time, rolling it round and round on his tongue until all the tang had gone. Then he placed the seed on the palm of his hand and studied it.

'Are cherry seeds lucky?' asked Rakesh.

'Of course.'

'Then I'll keep it.'

'Nothing is lucky if you put it away. If you want luck, you must put it to some use.

'What can I do with a seed?'

'Plant it.'

So Rakesh found a small space and began to dig up a flowerbed.

'Hey, not there,' said Grandfather. 'I've sown mustard in that bed. Plant it in that shady corner, where it won't be disturbed.'

Rakesh went to a corner of the garden where the earth was soft and yielding. He did not have to dig. He pressed the seed into the soil with his thumb and it went right in.

Then he had his lunch, and ran off to play cricket with his friends, and forgot all about the cherry seed.

When it was winter in the hills, a cold wind blew down from the snows and went *whoo-whoo-whoo* in the deodar trees, and the garden was dry and bare. In the evenings Grandfather and Rakesh sat over a charcoal fire, and Grandfather told Rakesh stories—stories about people who turned into animals, and ghosts who lived in trees, and beans that jumped and stones that wept—and in turn Rakesh would read to him from the newspaper, Grandfather's eyesight being rather weak. Rakesh found the newspaper very dull—especially after the stories—but Grandfather wanted all the news...

They knew it was spring when the wild duck flew north again, to Siberia. Early in the morning, when he got up to chop wood and light a fire, Rakesh saw the V-shaped formation streaming northward, the calls of the birds carrying clearly through the thin mountain air.

One morning in the garden he bent to pick up what he thought was a small twig and found to his surprise that it was well rooted. He stared at it for a moment, then ran to fetch Grandfather, calling, '*Dada*, come and look, the cherry tree has come up!'

'What cherry tree?' asked Grandfather, who had forgotten about it. 'The seed we planted last year—look, it's come up!'

Rakesh went down on his haunches, while Grandfather bent almost double and peered down at the tiny tree. It was about four inches high.

'Yes, it's a cherry tree,' said Grandfather. 'You should water it now and then.'

Rakesh ran indoors and came back with a bucket of water.

'Don't drown it!' said Grandfather.

Rakesh gave it a sprinkling and circled it with pebbles.

'What are the pebbles for?" asked Grandfather.

'For privacy,' said Rakesh.

He looked at the tree every morning but it did not seem to be growing very fast. So he stopped looking at it except quickly, out of the corner of his eye. And, after a week or two, when he allowed himself to look at it properly, he found that it had grown—at least an inch!

That year the monsoon rains came early and Rakesh plodded to and from school in raincoat and gumboots. Ferns sprang from the trunks of trees, strange-looking lilies came up in the long grass, and even when it wasn't raining the trees dripped and mist came curling up the valley. The cherry tree grew quickly in this season.

It was about two feet high when a goat entered the garden and ate all the leaves. Only the main stem and two thin branches remained.

'Never mind,' said Grandfather, seeing that Rakesh was upset. 'It will grow again, cherry trees are tough.'

Towards the end of the rainy season new leaves appeared on the tree. Then a woman cutting grass scrambled down the hillside, her scythe swishing through the heavy monsoon foliage. She did not try to avoid the tree: one sweep, and the cherry tree was cut in two.

When Grandfather saw what had happened, he went after the woman and scolded her; but the damage could not be repaired.

'Maybe it will die now,' said Rakesh.

'Maybe,' said Grandfather.

But the cherry tree had no intention of dying.

By the time summer came round again, it had sent out several new shoots with tender green leaves. Rakesh had grown taller too. He was eight now, a sturdy boy with curly black hair and deep black eyes. 'Blackberry eyes,' Grandfather called them.

That monsoon Rakesh went home to his village, to help his father and mother with the planting and ploughing and sowing. He was thinner but stronger when he came back to Grandfather's house at the end of the rain, to find that the cherry tree had grown another foot. It was now up to his chest.

Even when there was rain, Rakesh would sometimes water the tree. He wanted it to know that he was there.

One day he found a bright green praying-mantis perched on a branch, peering at him with bulging eyes. Rakesh let it remain there; it was the cherry tree's first visitor.

The next visitor was a hairy caterpillar, who started making a meal of the leaves. Rakesh removed it quickly and dropped it on a heap of dry leaves.

'Come back when you're a butterfly,' he said.

Winter came early. The cherry tree bent low with the weight of snow. Field-mice sought shelter in the roof of the cottage. The road from the valley was blocked, and for several days there was no newspaper, and this made Grandfather quite grumpy. His stories began to have unhappy endings.

In February it was Rakesh's birthday. He was nine—and the tree was four, but almost as tall as Rakesh.

One morning, when the sun came out, Grandfather came into the garden to 'let some warmth get into my bones,' as he put it. He stopped in front of the cherry tree, stared at it for a few moments, and then called out, 'Rakesh! Come and look! Come quickly before it falls!'

Rakesh and Grandfather gazed at the tree as though it had performed a miracle. There was a pale pink blossom at the end of a branch.

The following year there were more blossoms. And suddenly the tree was taller than Rakesh, even though it was less than half his age. And then it was taller than Grandfather, who was older than some of the oak trees.

But Rakesh had grown too. He could run and jump and climb trees as well as most boys, and he read a lot of books, although he still liked listening to Grandfather's tales.

In the cherry tree, bees came to feed on the nectar in the blossoms, and tiny birds pecked at the blossoms and broke them off. But the tree kept blossoming right through the spring, and there were always more blossoms than birds.

That summer there were small cherries on the tree. Rakesh tasted one and spat it out.

'It's too sour,' he said.

'They'll be better next year,' said Grandfather.

But the birds liked them—especially the bigger birds, such as the bulbuls and scarlet minivets—and they flitted in and out of the foliage, feasting on the cherries.

On a warm sunny afternoon, when even the bees looked sleepy, Rakesh was looking for Grandfather without finding him in any of his favourite places around the house. Then he looked out of the bedroom window and saw Grandfather reclining on a cane chair under the cherry tree.

'There's just the right amount of shade here,' said Grandfather. 'And I like looking at the leaves.'

'They're pretty leaves,' said Rakesh. 'And they are always ready to dance. If there's breeze.'

After Grandfather had come indoors, Rakesh went into the garden and lay down on the grass beneath the tree. He gazed up through the leaves at the great blue sky; and turning on his side, he could see the mountain striding away into the clouds. He was still lying beneath the tree when the evening shadows crept across the garden. Grandfather came back and sat down beside Rakesh, and they waited in silence until the stars came out and the nightjar began to call. In the forest below, the crickets and cicadas began tuning up; and suddenly the trees were full of the sound of insects.

'There are so many trees in the forest,' said Rakesh. 'What's so special about this tree? Why do we like it so much?'

'We planted it ourselves,' said Grandfather. That's why it's special.'

'Just one small seed,' said Rakesh, and he touched the smooth bark of the tree that had grown. He ran his hand along the trunk of the tree and put his finger to the tip of a leaf. 'I wonder,' he whispered. 'Is this what it feels to be God?'

From the Pool to the Glacier

1. My Boyhood Pool

It was going to rain. I could see the rain moving across the foothills, and I could smell it on the breeze. But instead of turning homewards I pushed my way through the leaves and brambles that grew across the forest path. I had heard the sound of running water at the bottom of the hill, and I was determined to find this hidden stream.

I had to slide down a rock-face into a small ravine and there I found the stream running over a bed of shingle, I removed my shoes and started walking upstream. A large glossy black bird with a curved red beak hooted at me as I passed; and a Paradise Flycatcher—this one I couldn't fail to recognise, with its long fan-tail beating the air—swooped across the stream. Water trickled down from the hillside, from amongst ferns and grasses and wild flowers; and the hills, rising steeply on either side, kept the ravine in shadow. The rocks were smooth, almost soft, and some of them were gray and some yellow. A small waterfall came down the rocks and formed a deep round pool of apple-green water.

When I saw the pool I turned and ran home. I wanted to tell Anil and Kamal about it. It began to rain, but I didn't stop to take shelter, I ran all the way home—through the *sal* forest, across the dry river-bed through the outskirts of the town.

Though Anil usually chose the adventures we were to have, the pool was my own discovery, and I was proud of it.

"We'll call it Rusty's Pool," said Kamal. "And remember, it's a secret pool. No one else must know of it."

I think it was the pool that brought us together more than anything else.

Kamal was the best swimmer. He dived off rocks and went gliding about under the water like a long golden fish. Anil had strong legs and arms, and he threshed about with much vigour but little skill. I could dive off a rock too, but I usually landed on my stomach.

There were slim silver fish in the stream. At first we tried catching them with a line, but they soon learnt the art of taking the bait without being caught on the hook. Next we tried a bedsheet (Anil had removed it from his mother's laundry) which we stretched across one end of the stream; but the fish wouldn't come anywhere near it. Eventually,

Anil without telling us, procured a stick of gunpowder. And Kamal and I were startled out of an afternoon siesta by a flash across the water and a deafening explosion. Half the hillside tumbled into the pool, and Anil along with it. We got him out, along with a large supply of stunned fish which were too small for eating. Anil, however, didn't want all his work to go to waste; so he roasted the fish over a fire and ate them himself.

The effects of the explosion gave Anil another idea, which was to enlarge our pool by building a dam across one end. This he accomplished with our combined labour. But he had chosen a week when there had been heavy rain in the hills, and we had barely finished the dam when a torrent of water came rushing down the bed of the stream and burst our earthworks, flooding the ravine. Our clothes were carried away by the current, and we had to wait until it was night before creeping into town through the darkest alley-ways. Anil was spotted at a street corner, but he posed as a naked Sadhu and began calling for alms, and finally slipped in through the back door of his house without being recognised. I had to lend Kamal some of my clothes, and these, being on the small side, made him look odd and gangly. Our other activities at the pool included wrestling and buffalo-riding.

We wrestled on a strip of sand that ran beside the stream. Anil had often attended wrestling *akharas* and was something of an expert. Kamal and I usually combined against him, and after five or ten minutes of furious unscientific struggle, we usually succeeded in flattening Anil into the sand. Kamal would sit on his head, and I would sit on his legs until he admitted defeat. There was no fun in taking him on singly, because he knew too many tricks for us.

We rode on a couple of buffaloes that sometimes came to drink and wallow in the more muddy parts of the stream. Buffaloes are fine, sluggish creatures, always in search of a soft, slushy resting place. We would climb on their backs, and kick and yell and urge them forward; but on no occasion did we succeed in getting them to carry us anywhere. If they tired of our antics, they would merely roll over on their backs, taking us with them into a bed of muddy water.

Not that it mattered how muddy we got, because we had only to dive into the pool to get rid of it all. The buffaloes couldn't get to the pool because of its narrow outlet and the slippery rocks.

If it was possible for Anil and me to leave our homes at night, we would come to the pool for a swim by moonlight. We would often find Kamal there before us. He wasn't afraid of the dark or the surrounding forest, where there were panthers and jungle cats. We bathed silently at nights, because the stillness of the surrounding jungle seemed to discourage high spirits; but sometimes Kamal would sing—he had a clear, ringing voice—and we would float the red, long-fingered poinsettias downstream.

The pool was to be our principal meeting-place during the coming months. It was not that we couldn't meet in town. But the pool was secret, known only to us, and it gave us a feeling of conspiracy and adventure to meet there after school. It was at the pool that we made our plans: it was at the pool that we first spoke of the Glacier: but several weeks and a few other exploits were to pass before the particular dream materialised.

2. Ghosts on the Verandah

Anil's mother's memory was stored with an incredible amount of folklore, and she would sometimes astonish us with her stories of spirits and mischievous ghosts.

One evening, when Anil's father was out of town, and Kamal and I had been invited to stay the night at Anil's upper-storey flat in the bazaar, his mother began to tell us about the various types of ghosts she had known. Mulia, a servant-girl, having just taken a bath, came out on the verandah, with her hair loose.

"My girl, you ought not to leave your hair loose like that," said Anil's mother. "It is better to tie a knot in it."

"But I have not oiled it yet," said Mulia.

"Never mind, but you should not leave your hair loose towards sunset. There are spirits called *jinns* who are attracted by long hair and pretty black eyes like yours. They may be tempted to carry you away!"

"How dreadful!" exclaimed Mulia, hurriedly tying a knot in her hair, and going indoors to be on the safe side.

Kamal, Anil and I sat on a string cot, facing Anil's mother, who sat on another cot. She was not much older than thirty-two, and had often been mistaken for Anil's elder sister; she came from a village near Mathura, a part of the country famous for its gods and spirits and demons.

"Can you see *Jinns*, aunty-ji?" I asked.

"Sometimes," she said. "There was an Urdu teacher in Mathura, whose pupils were about the same age as you. One of the boys was very good at his lessons. One day, while he sat at his desk in a corner of the classroom, the teacher asked him to fetch a book from the cupboard which stood at the far end of the room. The boy, who felt lazy that morning, didn't move from his seat. He merely stretched out his hand, took the book from the cupboard, and handed it to the teacher. Everyone was astonished, because the boy's arm had stretched about four yards before touching the book! They realised that he was a *jinn*; that was the reason for his being so good at games and exercises which required great agility."

"Well, I wish I was a *jinn*," said Anil. "Especially for volley-ball matches."

Anil's mother then told us about *Munjia*, a mischievous ghost who lives in lonely peepul trees. When a *Munjia* is annoyed, he rushes out from his tree and upsets tongas, bullock-carts and cycles. Even a bus is known to have been upset by a *Munjia*.

"If you are passing beneath a peepul tree at night," warned Anil's mother, "be careful not to yawn without covering your mouth or snapping your fingers in front of it. If you don't remember to do that, the *Munjia* will jump down your throat and completely ruin your digestion!"

In an attempt to change the subject, Kamal mentioned that a friend of his had found a snake in his bed one morning.

"Did he kill it?" asked Anil's mother anxiously.

"No, it slipped away," said Kamal.

"Good," she said. "It is lucky if you see a snake early in the morning."

"It won't bite you if you let it alone," she said.

By eleven o'clock, after we had finished our dinner and heard a few more ghost stories—including one about Anil's grandmother, whose spirit paid the family a visit—Kamal and I were most reluctant to leave the company on the verandah and retire to the room which had been set apart for us. It did not make us feel any better to be told by Anil's mother that we should recite certain magical verses to keep away the more mischievous spirits. We tried one, which went—

Bhoot, pret, pisach, dana
Chhoo mantar, sab nikal jana,
Mano, mano, Shiv ka kahna...
which, roughly translated, means—
Ghosts, spirits, goblins, sprites,
Away you fly, don't come tonight,
Or with great Shiva you'll have to fight!

Shiva, the Destroyer, is one of the three major Hindu deities.

But the more we repeated the verse, the more uneasy we became, and when I got into bed (after carefully examining it for snakes), I couldn't lie still, but kept twisting and turning and looking at the walls for moving shadows. Kamal attempted to raise our spirits by singing softly, but this only made the atmosphere more eerie. After a while we heard someone knocking at the door, and the voices of Anil and the maidservant. Getting up and opening the door, I found them looking pale and anxious. They, too, had succeeded in frightening themselves as a result of Anil's mother's stories.

"Are you all right?" asked Anil. "Wouldn't you like to sleep in our part of the house? It might be safer. Mulia will help us to carry the beds across!"

"We're quite all right," protested Kamal and I, refusing to admit we were nervous; but we were hustled along to the other side of the flat as though a band of ghosts was conspiring against us. Anil's mother had been absent during all this activity but suddenly we heard her screaming from the direction of the room we had just left.

"Rusty and Kamal have disappeared!" she cried. "Their beds have gone, too!"

And then, when she came out on the verandah and saw us dashing about in our pyjamas, she gave another scream and collapsed on a cot.

After that, we didn't allow Anil's mother to tell us ghost stories at night.

3. To the Hills

At the end of August, when the rains were nearly over, we met at the pool to make plans for the autumn holidays. We had bathed, and were stretched out in the shade of the fresh, rain-washed *sal* trees, when Kamal, pointing vaguely to the distant mountains, said: "Why don't we go to the Pindari Glacier?"

"The Glacier!" exclaimed Anil. "But that's all snow and ice!"

"Of course it is," said Kamal. "But there's a path through the mountains that goes all the way to the foot of the glacier. It's only fifty-four miles!"

"Do you mean we must—*walk* fifty-four miles?"

"Well, there's no other way," said Kamal. "Unless you prefer to sit on a mule. But your legs are too long, they'll be trailing along the ground. No, we'll have to walk. It will take us about ten days to get to the glacier and back, but if we take enough food there'll be no problem. There are *dak* bungalows to stay in at night."

"Kamal gets all the best ideas," I said. "But I suppose Anil and I will have to get our parents' permission. And some money."

"My mother won't let me go," said Anil. "She says the mountains are full of ghosts. And she thinks I'll get up to some mischief. How can one get up to mischief on a lonely mountain?"

"I'm sure it won't be dangerous, people are always going to the glacier. Can you see that peak above the others on the right?" Kamal pointed to the distant snow-range, barely visible against the soft blue sky. "The Pindari Glacier is below it. It's at 12,000 feet, I think, but we won't need any special equipment. There'll be snow only for the final two or three miles. Do you know that it's the beginning of the river Sarayu?"

"You mean our river?" asked Anil, thinking of the little river that wandered along the outskirts of the town, joining the Ganges further downstream.

"Yes. But it's only a trickle where it starts."

"How much money will we need?" I asked, determined to be practical.

"Well, I've saved twenty rupees," said Kamal.

"But won't you need that for your books?" I asked.

"No, this is extra. If each of us brings twenty rupees, we should have enough. There's nothing to spend money on, once we are up on the mountains. There are only one or two villages on the way, and food is scarce, so we'll have to take plenty of food with us. I learnt all this from the Tourist Office."

"Kamal's been planing this without our knowledge," complained Anil.

"He always plans in advance," I said. "but it's a good idea, and it should be a fine adventure."

"All right," said Anil. "But Rusty will have to be with me when I ask my mother. She thinks Rusty is very sensible, and might let me go if he says it's quite safe." And he ended the discussion by jumping into the pool, where we soon joined him.

Though my mother hesitated about letting me go, my father said it was a wonderful idea, and was only sorry because he couldn't accompany us himself (which was a relief, as we didn't want our parents along); and though Anil's father hesitated—or rather, because he hesitated—his mother said yes, of course Anil must go, the mountain air would be good for his health. A puzzling remark, because Anil's health had never been better. The bazaar people, when they heard that Anil might be away for a couple of weeks, were overjoyed at the prospect of a quiet spell, and pressed his father to let him go.

On a cloudy day, promising rain, we bundled ourselves into the bus that was to take us to Kapkote (where people lose their caps and coats, punned Anil), the starting point of our trek. Each of us carried a haversack, and we had also brought along a good-sized bedding-roll which, apart from blankets, also contained rice and flour thoughtfully provided by Anil's mother. We had no idea how we would carry the bedding-roll once we started walking; but an astrologer had told Anil's mother it was a good day for travelling, so we didn't worry much over minor details.

We were soon in the hills, on a winding road that took us up and up, until we saw the valley and our town spread out beneath us, the river a silver ribbon across the plain. Kamal pointed to a patch of dense *sal* forest and said, "Our pool must be there!" We took a sharp bend, and the valley disappeared, and the mountains towered above us.

We had dull headaches by the time we reached Kapkote; but when we got down from the bus a cool breeze freshened us. At the wayside shop we drank glasses of hot, sweet tea, and the shopkeeper told us we could spend the night in one of his rooms. It was pleasant at Kapkote, the hills wooded with deodar trees, the lower slopes planted with fresh green paddy. At night there was a wind moaning in the trees, and it found its way through the cracks in the windows and eventually through our blankets. Then, right outside the door, a dog began howling at the moon. It had been a good day for travelling, but the astrologer hadn't warned us that it would be a bad night for sleep.

Next morning we washed our faces at a small stream about a hundred yards from the shop, and filled our water-bottles for the day's march. A boy from the nearby village sat on a rock, studying our movements.

"Where are you going?" he asked, unable to suppress his curiosity.

"To the glacier," said Kamal.

"Let me come with you," said the boy. "I know the way."

"You're too small," said Anil. "We need someone who can carry our bedding-roll."

"I'm small," said the boy, "but I'm strong. I'm not a weakling like the boys in the plains." Though he was shorter than any of us, he certainly looked sturdy, and had a muscular well-knit body and pink cheeks. "See!" he said; and picking up a rock the size of a football, he heaved it across the stream.

"I think he can come with us," I said.

And the boy, whose name was Bisnu, dashed off to inform his people of his employment—we had agreed to pay him a rupee a day for acting as our guide and 'sherpa'.

And then we were walking—at first, above the little Sarayu river, then climbing higher along the rough mule-track, always within sound of the water. Kamal wanted to bathe in the river. I said it was too far, and Anil said we wouldn't reach the dak bungalow before dark if we went for a swim. Regretfully, we left the river behind, and marched on through a forest of oaks, over wet, rotting leaves that made a soft carpet for our feet. We ate at noon, under an oak. As we didn't want to waste any time making a fire— not on this first crucial day—we ate beans from a tin and drank most of our water.

In the afternoon we came to the river again. The water was swifter now, green and bubbling, still far below us. We saw two boys in the water, swimming in an inlet which reminded us of our own secret pool. They waved, and invited us to join them. We returned their greeting; but it would have taken us an hour to get down to the river and up again; so we continued on our way.

We walked fifteen miles on the first day—our speed was to decrease after this—and we were at the *dak* bungalow by six o'clock. Bisnu busied himself collecting sticks for a fire. Anil found the bungalow's watchman asleep in a patch of fading sunlight, and roused him. The watchman, who hadn't been bothered by visitors for weeks, grumbled at our intrusion, but opened a room for us. He also produced some potatoes from his quarters, and these were roasted for dinner.

It became cold after the sun had gone down, and we remained close to Bisnu's fire. The damp sticks burnt fitfully.

But Bisnu had justified his inclusion in our party. He had balanced the bedding-roll on his shoulders as though it were full of cotton wool instead of blankets. Now he was helping with the cooking. And we were glad to have him sharing our hot potatoes and strong tea.

There were only two beds in the room, and we pushed these together, apportioning out the blankets as fairly as possible. Then the four of us leapt into bed, shivering in the cold. We were already over 5,000 feet. Bisnu, in his own peculiar way, had wrapped a scarf round his neck, though a cotton singlet and shorts were all that he wore for the night.

"Tell us a story, Rusty," said Anil. "It will help us to fall asleep."

I told them one of his mother's stories, about a boy and a girl who had been changed into a pair of buffaloes; and then Bisnu told us about the ghost of a Sadhu, who was to be seen sitting in the snow by moonlight, not far from the glacier. Far from putting us to sleep, this story kept us awake for hours.

"Aren't you asleep yet?" I asked Anil in the middle of the night.

"No, you keep kicking me," he lied.

"We don't have enough blankets," complained Kamal, "It's too cold to sleep."

"I never sleep till it's very late," mumbled Bisnu from the bottom of the bed.

No one was prepared to admit that our imaginations were keeping us awake.

After a little while we heard a thud on the corrugated tin sheeting, and then the sound of someone—or something—scrambling about on the roof. Anil, Kamal and I sat up in bed, startled out of our wits. Bisnu, who had been winning the race to be fast asleep, merely turned over on his side and grunted.

"It's only a bear," he said. "Didn't you notice the pumpkins on the roof? Bears love pumpkins."

For half an hour we had to listen to the bear as it clambered about on the roof, feasting on the watchman's ripening pumpkins. Finally there was silence. Kamal and I crawled out of our blankets and went to the window. And through the frosted glass we saw a black Himalayan bear ambling across the slope in front of the bungalow, a fat pumpkin held between its paws.

4. To The River

It was raining when we woke, and the mountains were obscured by a heavy mist. We delayed our departure, playing football on the verandah with one of the pumpkins that had fallen off the roof. At noon the rain stopped, and the sun shone through the clouds. As the mist lifted, we saw the snow range, the great peaks of Nanda Kot and Trisul stepping into the sky.

"It's different up here," said Kamal. "I feel a different person."

"That's the altitude," I said. "As we go higher, we'll get lighter in the head."

"Anil is light in the head already," said Kamal. "I hope the altitude isn't too much for him."

"If you two are going to be witty," said Anil, "I shall go off with Bisnu, and you'll have to find the way yourselves."

Bisnu grinned at each of us in turn to show us that he wasn't taking sides; and after a breakfast of boiled eggs, we set off on our trek to the next bungalow.

Rain had made the ground slippery, and we were soon ankle-deep in slush. Our next bungalow lay in a narrow valley, on the banks of the rushing Pindar river, which twisted its way through the mountains. We were not sure how far we had to go, but nobody seemed in a hurry. On an impulse, I decided to hurry on ahead of the others. I wanted to be waiting for them at the river.

The path dropped steeply, then rose and went round a big mountain. I met a woodcutter and asked him how far it was to the river. He was a short, stocky man, with gnarled hands and a weathered face.

"Seven miles," he said. "Are you alone?"

"No, the others are following, but I cannot wait for them. If you meet them, tell them I'll be waiting at the river."

The path descended steeply now, and I had to run a little. It was a dizzy, winding path. The hillside was covered with lush green ferns, and, in the trees, unseen birds sang loudly. Soon I was in the valley, and the path straightened out. A girl was coming from the opposite direction. She held a long, curved knife, with which she had been cutting grass and fodder. There were rings in her nose and ears, and her arms were covered with heavy bangles. The bangles made music when she moved her hands—it was as though her hands spoke a language of their own.

"How far is it to the river?" I asked.

The girl had probably never been near the river, or she may have been thinking of another one, because she replied, "Twenty miles," without any hesitation.

I laughed, and ran down the path. A parrot screeched suddenly, flew low over my head—a flash of blue and green—and took the course of the path, while I followed its dipping flight, until the path rose and the bird disappeared into the trees.

A trickle of water came from the hillside, and I stopped to drink. The water was cold and sharp and very refreshing. I had walked alone for nearly an hour. Presently I saw a boy ahead of me, driving a few goats along the path.

"How far is it to the river?" I asked, when I caught up with him.

The boy said, "Oh, not far, just round the next hill."

As I was hungry, I produced some dry bread from my pocket and, breaking it in two, offered half to the boy. We sat on the grassy hillside and ate in silence. Then we walked on together and began talking; and talking, I did not notice the smarting of my feet and the distance I had covered. But after some time the boy had to diverge along another path, and I was once more on my own.

I missed the village boy. I looked up and down the path, but I could see no one, no sign of Anil and Kamal and

Bisnu, and the river was not in sight either. I began to feel discouraged. But I couldn't turn back; I was determined to be at the river before the others.

And so I walked on, along the muddy path, past terraced fields and small stone houses, until there were no more fields and houses, only forest and sun and silence.

The silence was impressive and a little frightening. It was different from the silence of a room or an empty street. Nor was there any movement, except for the bending of grass beneath my feet, and the circling of a hawk high above the fir trees.

And then, as I rounded a sharp bend, the silence broke into sound.

The sound of the river.

Far down in the valley, the river tumbled over itself in its impatience to reach the plains. I began to run, slipped and stumbled, but continued running.

And the water was blue and white and wonderful.

When Anil, Kamal and Bisnu arrived, the four of us bravely decided to bathe in the little river. The late afternoon sun was still warm, but the water—so clear and inviting—proved to be ice-cold. Only twenty miles upstream the river emerged as a little trickle from the glacier, and in its swift descent down the mountain slopes it did not give the sun a chance to penetrate its waters. But we were determined to bathe, to wash away the dust and sweat of our two days' trudging, and we leapt about in the shallows like startled porpoises, slapping water on each other, and gasping with the shock of each immersion. Bisnu, more accustomed to mountain streams than ourselves, ventured across in an attempt to catch an otter, but wasn't fast enough. Then we were on the springy grass, wrestling each other in order to get warm.

The bungalow stood on a ledge just above the river, and the sound of the water rushing down the mountain defile could be heard at all times. The sound of the birds, which we had grown used to, was drowned by the sound of the water; but the birds themselves could be seen, many-coloured, standing out splendidly against the dark green forest foliage: the red-crowned jay, the paradise flycatcher, the purple whistling-thrush, others we could not recognise.

Higher up the mountain, above some terraced land where oats and barley were grown, stood a small cluster of huts. This, we were told by the watchman, was the last village on the way to the glacier. It was, in fact, one of the last villages in India, because if we crossed the difficult passes beyond the glacier, we would find ourselves in Tibet. We told the watchman we would be quite satisfied if we reached the glacier.

Then Anil made the mistake of mentioning the Abominable Snowman, of whom we had been reading in the papers. The people of Nepal believe in the existence of the Snowman, and our watchman was a Nepali.

"Yes, I have seen the Yeti," he told us. "A great shaggy flat-footed creature. In the winter, when it snows heavily, he passes by the bungalow at night. I have seen his tracks the next morning."

"Does he come this way in the summer?" I asked anxiously. We were sitting before another of Bisnu's fires, drinking tea with condensed milk, and trying to get through a black, sticky sweet which the watchman had produced from his tin trunk.

"The yeti doesn't come here in the summer," said the old man. "But I have seen the Lidini sometimes. You have to be careful of her."

"What is a Lidini?" asked Kamal.

"Ah!" said the watchman mysteriously. "You have heard of the Abominable Snowman, no doubt, but there are few who have heard of the Abominable Snowwoman! And yet she is far the more dangerous of the two!"

"What is she like?" asked Anil, and we all craned forward.

"She is of the same height as the Yeti—about seven feet when her back is straight—and her hair is much longer. She has very long teeth and nails. Her feet face inwards, but she can run very fast, especially downhill. If you see a Lidini, and she chases you, always run away in an uphill direction. She tires quickly because of her feet. But when running downhill she has no trouble at all, and you have to be very fast to escape her!"

"Well, we're all good runners," said Anil with a nervous laugh, "but it's just a fairy story, I don't believe a word of it."

"But you *must* believe fairy stories," I said, remembering a performance of Peter Pan in London, when those in the audience who believed in fairies were asked to clap their hands in order to save Tinker Bell's life. "Even if they aren't true," I added, deciding there was a world of difference between Tinker Bell and the Abominable Snowwoman.

"Well, I don't believe there's a Snowman or a Snowwoman!" declared Anil.

The watchman was most offended and refused to tell us anything about the Sagpa and Sagpani; but Bisnu knew about them, and later, when we were in bed, he told us that they were similar to Snowmen but much smaller. Their favourite pastime was sleeping, and they became very annoyed if anyone woke them, and became ferocious, and did not give one much time to start running uphill. The Sagpa and Sagpani sometimes kidnapped small children, and taking them to their cave, would look after the children very carefully, feeding them on fruits, honey, rice and earthworms.

"When the Sagpa isn't looking," he said, "you can throw the earthworms over your shoulder."

5. The Glacier

It was a fine sunny morning when we set out to cover the last seven miles to the glacier. We had expected this to be a stiff climb, but the last dak bungalow was situated at well over 10,000 feet above sea level, and the ascent was to be fairly gradual.

And suddenly, abruptly, there were no more trees. As the bungalow dropped out of sight, the trees and bushes gave way to short grass and little blue and pink alpine

From the Pool to the Glacier

flowers. The snow peaks were close now, ringing us in on every side. We passed waterfalls, cascading hundreds of feet down precipitous rock faces, thundering into the little river. A great golden eagle hovered over us for some time.

"I feel different again," said Kamal.

"We're very high now," I said. "I hope we won't get headaches."

"I've got one already," complained Anil. "Let's have some tea."

We had left our cooking utensils at the bungalow, expecting to return there for the night, and had brought with us only a few biscuits, chocolate, and a thermos of tea. We finished the tea, and Bisnu scrambled about on the grassy slopes, collecting wild strawberries. They were tiny strawberries, very sweet, and they did nothing to satisfy our appetites. There was no sign of habitation or human life. The only creatures to be found at that height were the gurals—sure-footed mountain goats—and an occasional snow-leopard, or a bear.

We found and explored a small cave, and then, turning a bend, came unexpectedly upon the glacier.

The hill fell away, and there, confronting us, was a great white field of snow and ice, cradled between two peaks that could only have been the abode of the gods. We were speechless for several minutes. Kamal took my hand and held on to it for reassurance; perhaps he was not sure that what he saw was real. Anil's mouth hung open. Bisnu's eyes glittered with excitement.

We proceeded cautiously on the snow, supporting each other on the slippery surface; but we could not go far, because we were quite unequipped for any high-altitude climbing. It was pleasant to feel that we were the only boys in our town who had climbed so high. A few black rocks jutted out from the snow, and we sat down on them, to feast our eyes on the view. The sun reflected sharply from the snow, and we felt surprisingly warm.

"Let's sunbathe!" said Anil, on a sudden impulse.

"Yes, let's do that!" I said.

In a few minutes we had taken off our clothes and, sitting on the rocks, were exposing ourselves to the elements. It was delicious to feel the sun crawling over my skin. Within half an hour I was post box red, and so was Bisnu, and the two of us decided to get into our clothes before the sun scorched the skin off our backs. Kamal and Anil appeared to be more resilient to sunlight, and laughed at our discomfiture. Bisnu and I avenged ourselves by gathering up handfuls of snow and rubbing it on their backs. We dressed quickly enough after that, Anil leaping about like a performing monkey.

Meanwhile, almost imperceptibly, clouds had covered some of the peaks, and white mist drifted down the mountain-slopes. It was time to get back to the bungalow; we would barely make it before dark.

We had not gone far when lightning began to sizzle about the mountain-tops followed by waves of thunder.

"Let's run!" shouted Anil. "We can shelter in the cave!"

The clouds could hold themselves in no longer, and the rain came down suddenly, stinging our faces as it was whipped up by an icy wind. Half-blinded, we ran as fast as we could along the slippery path, and stumbled, drenched and exhausted, into the little cave.

The cave was mercifully dry, and not very dark. We remained at the entrance, watching the rain sweep past us, listening to the wind whistling down the long gorge.

"It will take some time to stop," said Kamal.

"No, it will pass soon," said Bisnu. "These storms are short and fierce."

Anil produced his pocket knife, and to pass the time we carved our names in the smooth rock of the cave.

"We will come here again, when we are older," said Kamal, "and perhaps our names will still be here."

It had grown dark by the time the rain stopped. A full moon helped us find our way, we went slowly and carefully. The rain had loosened the earth, and stones kept rolling down the hillside. I was afraid of starting a landslide.

"I hope we don't meet the Lidini now," said Anil fervently.

"I thought you didn't believe in her," I said.

"I don't," replied Anil. "But what if I'm wrong?"

We saw only a mountain-goat, the gural, poised on the brow of a precipice, silhouetted against the sky.

And then the path vanished.

Had it not been for the bright moonlight, we might have walked straight into an empty void. The rain had caused a landslide, and where there had been a narrow path there was now only a precipice of loose, slippery shale.

"We'll have to go back," said Bisnu. "It will be too dangerous to try and cross in the dark."

"We'll sleep in the cave," I suggested.

"We've nothing to sleep in," said Anil. "Not a single blanket between us and nothing to eat!"

"We'll just have to rough it till morning," said Kamal. "It will be better than breaking our necks here."

We returned to the cave, which did at least have the virtue of being dry. Bisnu had matches, and he made a fire with some dry sticks which had been left in the cave by a previous party. We ate what was left of a loaf of bread.

There was no sleep for any of us that night. We lay close to each other for comfort, but the ground was hard and uneven. And every noise we heard outside the cave made us think of leopards and bears and even the Abominable Snowmen.

We got up as soon as there was a faint glow in the sky. The snow-peaks were bright pink, but we were too tired and hungry and worried to care for the beauty of the sunrise. We took the path to the landslide, and once again looked for a way across. Kamal ventured to take a few steps on the loose pebbles, but the ground gave way immediately, and we had to grab him by the arms and shoulders to prevent him from sliding a hundred feet down the gorge.

"Now what are we going to do?" I asked.

"Look for another way," said Bisnu.

"But do you know of any?"

And we all turned to look at Bisnu, expecting him to provide the solution to our problem.

"I have heard of a way," said Bisnu, "but I have never used it. It will be a little dangerous, I think. The path has not been used for several years—not since the traders stopped coming in from Tibet."

"Never mind, we'll try it," said Anil.

"We will have to cross the glacier first," said Bisnu. "That's the main problem."

We looked at each other in silence. The glacier didn't look difficult to cross, but we know that it would not be easy for novices. For almost two furlongs it consisted of hard, slippery ice.

Anil was the first to arrive at a decision.

"Come on," he said. "There's no time to waste."

We were soon on the glacier. And we remained on it for a long time. For every two steps forward, we slid one step backward. Our progress was slow and awkward. Sometimes, after advancing several yards across the ice at a steep incline, one of us would slip back and the others would have to slither down to help him up. At one particularly difficult spot, I dropped our water bottle and, grabbing at it, lost my footing, fell full-length and went sliding some twenty feet down the ice-slope.

I had sprained my wrist and hurt my knee, and was to prove a liability for the rest of the trek.

Kamal tied his handkerchief round my hand, and Anil took charge of the water-bottle, which we had filled with ice. Using my good hand to grab Bisnu's legs whenever I slipped, I struggled on behind the others.

It was almost noon, and we were quite famished, when we put our feet on grass again. And then we had another steep climb, clutching at roots and grasses, before we reached the path that Bisnu had spoken about. It was little more than a goat-track, but it took us round the mountain and brought us within sight of the *dak* bungalow.

"I could eat a whole chicken," said Kamal.

"I could eat two," I said.

"I could eat a Snowman," said Bisnu.

"And I could eat the chowkidar," said Anil.

Fortunately for the chowkidar, he had anticipated our hunger; and when we staggered into the bungalow late in the afternoon, we found a meal waiting for us. True, there was no chicken—but, so ravenous did we feel, that even the lowly onion tasted delicious!

We had Bisnu to thank for getting us back successfully. He had brought us over mountain and glacier with all the skill and confidence of a boy who had the Himalayas in his blood.

We took our time getting back to Kapkote; fished in the Sarayu river; bathed with the village boys we had seen on our way up; collected straw-berries and ferns and wild flowers; and finally said good-bye to Bisnu.

Anil wanted to take Bisnu along with us, but the boy's parents refused to let him go, saying that he was too young for the life of a city; but we were of the opinion that Bisnu could have taught the city boys a few things.

"Never mind," said Kamal. "We'll go on another trip next year, and we'll take you with us, Bisnu. We'll write and let you know our plans."

This promise made Bisnu happy, and he saw us off at the bus stop, shouldering our bedding to the end. Then he skimmed up the trunk of a fir tree to have a better view of us leaving, and we saw him waving to us from the tree as our bus went round the bend from Kapkote, and the hills were left behind and the plains stretched out below.

The Last Truck Ride

[*Twice a day Pritam Singh takes his battered, old truck on the narrow, mountainous roads, to the limestone quarry. He is in the habit of driving fast. The brakes of his truck are in good condition. What happens when a stray mule suddenly appears on the road?*]

A horn blared, shattering the silence of the mountains, and a truck came round the bend in the road. A herd of goats scattered to left and right.

The goat-herds cursed as a cloud of dust enveloped them, and then the truck had left them behind and was rattling along the stony, unpaved hill road.

At the wheel of the truck, stroking his gray moustache, sat Pritam Singh, a turbaned Sikh. It was his own truck. He did not allow anyone else to drive it. Everyday he made two trips to the limestone quarries, carrying truckloads of limestone back to the depot at the bottom of the hill. He was paid by the trip, and he was always anxious to get in two trips everyday.

Sitting beside him was Nathu, his cleaner-boy. Nathu was a sturdy boy, with a round cheerful face. It was difficult to guess his age. He might have been twelve or he might have been fifteen—he did not know himself, since no one in his village had troubled to record his birthday—but the hard life he led probably made him look older than his years. He belonged to the hills, but his village was far away, on the next range.

Last year the potato crop had failed. As a result there was no money for salt, sugar, soap and flour—and Nathu's parents, and small brothers and sisters couldn't live entirely on the onions and artichokes which were about the only crops that had survived the drought. There had been no rain that summer. So Nathu waved good-bye to his people and came down to the town in the valley to look for work. Someone directed him to the limestone depot. He was too young to work at the quarries, breaking stones and loading them on the trucks; but Pritam Singh, one of the older drivers, was looking for someone to clean and look after his truck. Nathu looked like a bright, strong boy, and he was taken on—at ten rupees a day.

That had been six months ago, and now Nathu was an experienced hand at looking after trucks, riding in them and even sleeping in them. He got on well with Pritam

Singh, the grizzled, fifty-year-old Sikh, who had well-to-do sons in the Punjab, but whose sturdy independence kept him on the road in his battered old truck.

Pritam Singh pressed hard on his horn. Now there was no one on the road—no animals, no humans—but Pritam was fond of his horn and liked blowing it. It was music to his ears.

'One more year on this road,' said Pritam. 'Then I'll sell my truck and retire.'

'Who will buy this truck? said Nathu. 'It will retire before you do.' 'Don't be cheeky, boy. She's only twenty-years-old—there are still a few years left in her! And as though to prove it, he blew his horn again. Its strident sound echoed and re-echoed down the mountain gorge. A pair of wild fowl, disturbed by the noise, flew out from the bushes and glided across the road in front of the truck.

Pritam Singh's thoughts went to his dinner.

'Haven't had a good meal for days,' he grumbled.

'Haven't had a good meal for weeks,' said Nathu, although he looked quite well-fed.

'Tomorrow I'll give you dinner,' said Pritam. 'Tandoori chicken and pilaf rice.'

'I'll believe it when I see it,' said Nathu.

Pritam Singh sounded his horn again before slowing down. The road had become narrow and precipitous, and trotting ahead of them was a train of mules. As the horn blared, one mule ran forward, one ran backwards. One went uphill, one went downhill. Soon there were mules all over the place.

'You can never tell with mules,' said Pritam, after he had left them behind.

The hills were bare and dry. Much of the forest had long since disappeared. Just a few scraggy old oaks still grew on the steep hillside. This particular range was rich in limestone, and the hills were scarred by quarrying.

'Are your hills as bare as these?' asked Pritam.

'No, they have not started blasting there as yet,' said Nathu.

'We still have a few trees. And there is a walnut tree in front of our house, which gives us two baskets of walnuts every year'.

'And do you have water?'

'There is a stream at the bottom of the hill. But for the fields, we have to depend on the rainfall. And there was no rain last year.'

'It will rain soon.' said Pritam. 'I can smell rain. It is coming from the north.'

'It will settle the dust.'

The dust was everywhere. The truck was full of it. The leaves of the shrubs and the few trees were thick with it. Nathu could feel the dust near his eyelids and on his lips. As they approached the quarries, the dust increased—but it was a different kind of dust now—whiter, stinging the eyes, irritating the nostrils—limestone dust, hanging in the air.

The blasting was in progress.

Pritam Singh brought the truck to a halt.

'Let's wait a bit,' he said.

They sat in silence, staring through the windscreen at the scarred cliffs about a hundred yards down the road. There was no sign of life around them.

Suddenly, the hillside blossomed outwards, followed by a sharp crack of explosives. Earth and rock hurtled down the hillside.

Nathu watched in awe as shrubs and small trees were flung into the air. It always frightened him—not so much the sight of the rocks bursting asunder, but the trees being flung aside and destroyed. He thought of his own trees at home—the walnut, the pines—and wondered if one day they would suffer the same fate, and whether the mountains would all become a desert like this particular range. No trees, no grass, no water—only the choking dust of the limestone quarries.

Pritam Singh pressed hard on his horn again, to let the people at the site know he was coming. Soon they were parked outside a small shed, where the contractor and the overseer were sipping cups of tea. A short distance away some labourers were hammering at chunks of rock, breaking them up into manageable blocks. A pile of stones stood ready for loading, while the rock that had just been blasted lay scattered about the hillside.

'Come and have a cup of tea,' called out the contractor.

'Get on with the loading,' said Pritam. 'I can't hang about all afternoon. There's another trip to make—and it gets dark early these days.'

But he sat down on a bench and ordered two cups of tea from the stall-owner. The overseer strolled over to the group of labourers and told them to start loading. Nathu let down the grid at the back of the truck.

Nathu stood back while the men loaded the truck with limestone rocks. He was glad that he was chubby: thin people seemed to feel the cold much more—like the contractor, a skinny fellow who was shivering in his expensive overcoat.

To keep himself warm, Nathu began helping the labourers with the loading.

'Don't expect to be paid for that,' said the contractor, for whom every extra paise spent was a paisa off his profits.

'Don't worry,' said Nadhu, 'I don't work for contractors. I work for Pritam Singh.'

'That's right,' called out Pritam. 'And mind what you say to Nathu—he's nobody's servant!'

It took them almost an hour to fill the truck with stones. The contractor wasn't happy until there was no space left for a single stone. Then four of the six labourers climbed on the pile of stones. They would ride back to the depot on the truck. The contractor, his overseer, and the others would follow by jeep. 'Let's go!' said Pritam, getting behind the steering wheel. 'I want to be back here and then home by eight o'clock. I'm going to a marriage party tonight!'

Nathu jumped in beside him, banging his door shut. It never opened at a touch. Pritam always joked that his truck was held together with Sellotape.

He was in good spirits. He started his engine, blew his horn, and burst into a song as the truck started out on the return journey.

The labourers were singing too, as the truck swung round the sharp bends of the winding mountain road. Nathu was feeling quite dizzy. The door beside him rattled on its hinges.

'Not so fast,' he said.

'Oh,' said Pritam, 'And since when did you become nervous about fast driving?'

'Since today,' said Nathu.

'And what's wrong with today?'

'I don't know. It's just that kind of day, I suppose.'

'You are getting old,' said Pritam. That's your trouble.'

'Just wait till you get to be my age,' said Nathu.

'No more cheek,' said Pritam, and stepped on the accelerator and drove faster.

As they swung round a bend, Nathu looked out of his window.

All he saw was the sky above and the valley below.

They were very near the edge. But it was always like that on this narrow road.

After a few more hairpin bends, the road started descending steeply to the valley.

'I'll just test the brakes,' said Pritam and jammed down on them so suddenly that one of the labourers almost fell off at the back.

They called out in protest.

'Hang on!' shouted Pritam. 'You're nearly home!'

'Don't try any short cuts,' said Nathu.

Just then a stray mule appeared in the middle of the road. Pritam swung the steering wheel over to his right; but the road turned left, and the truck went straight over the edge.

As it tipped over, hanging for a few seconds on the edge of the cliff, the labourers leapt from the back of the truck.

'The truck pitched forward, bouncing over the rocks, turning over on its side and rolling over twice before coming to rest against the trunk of a scraggy old oak tree. Had it missed the tree, the truck would have plunged a few hundred feet down to the bottom of the gorge.

Two labourers sat on the hillside, stunned and badly shaken.

The other two had picked themselves up and were running back to the quarry for help.

Nathu had landed in a bed of nettles. He was smarting all over, but he wasn't really hurt.

His first impulse was to get up and run back with the labourers. Then he realized that Pritam was still in the truck. If he wasn't dead, he would certainly be badly injured.

Nathu skidded down the steep slope, calling out, 'Pritam, Pritam, are you all right?

There was no answer.

Then he saw Pritam's arm and half his body jutting out of the open door of the truck. It was a strange position to be in, half in and half out. When Nathu came nearer, he saw Pritam was jammed in the driver's seat, held there by the steering wheel which was pressed hard against his chest. Nathu thought he was dead. But as he was about to turn away and clamber back up the hill, he saw Pritam open one blackened swollen eye. It looked straight up at Nathu.

'Are you alive?' whispered Nathu, terrified.

'What do you think?' muttered Pritam.

He closed his eye again.

When the contractor and his men arrived, it took them almost an hour to get him to a hospital in the town. He had a broken collarbone, a dislocated shoulder, and several fractured ribs. But the doctors said he was repairable—which was more than could be said for his truck.

'The truck's finished,' said Pritam, when Nathu came to see him a few days later. 'Now 'I'll have to go home and live with my sons. But you can get work on another truck.'

'No,' said Nathu. 'I'm gong home too.'

'And what will you do there?'

'I'll work on the land. It's better to grow things on the land than to blast things out of it.'

They were silent for some time.

'Do you know something?' said Pritam finally. 'But for that tree, the truck would have ended up at the bottom of the hill and I wouldn't be here, all bandaged up and talking to you. It was the tree that saved me. Remember that, boy.'

I'll remember,' said Nathu.

A Walk through Garhwal

I wake to what sounds like the din of a factory buzzer, but is in fact the music of a single vociferous cicada in the lime tree near my window.

Through the open window, I focus on a pattern of small, glossy lime leaves; then through them I see the mountains, the Himalayas, striding away into an immensity of sky.

"In a thousand ages of the gods I could not tell thee of the glories of Himachal". So confessed a Sanskrit poet at the dawn of Indian history and he came closer than anyone else to capturing the spell of the Himalayas. The sea has had Conrad and Stevenson and Masefield, but the mountains continue to defy the written word. We have climbed their highest peaks and crossed their most difficult passes, but still they keep their secrets and their reserve; they remain remote, mysterious, spirit-haunted.

No wonder then, that the people who live on the mountain slopes in the mist-filled valleys of Garhwal, have long since learned humility, patience and a quiet resignation. Deep in the crouching mist lie their villages, while climbing the mountain slopes are forests of rhododendron, spruce and deodar, soughing in the wind from the ice-bound passes. Pale women plough, they laugh at the thunder as their men go down to the plains for work; for little grows on the beautiful mountains in the north wind.

When I think of Manjari village in Garhwal I see a small river, a tributary of the Ganga, rushing along the bottom of a steep, rocky valley. On the banks of the river and on the terraced hills above, there are small fields of corn, barley, mustard, potatoes and onions. A few fruit trees grow near the village. Some hillsides are rugged and bare, just masses of quartz or granite. On hills exposed to wind, only grass and small shrubs are able to obtain a foothold.

This landscape is typical of Garhwal, one of India's most northerly regions with its massive snow ranges bordering on Tibet. Although thinly populated it does not provide much of a living for its people. Most Garhwali cultivators are poor, some are very poor. "You have beautiful scenery," I observed after crossing the first range of hills.

"Yes," said my friend, "but we cannot eat the scenery."

And yet these are cheerful people, sturdy and with wonderful powers of endurance. Somehow they manage to wrest a precarious living from the unhelpful, calcinated soil. I am their guest for a few days.

A Walk through Garhwal

My friend Gajadhar has brought me to his home, to his village above the little Nayar river. We took a train into the foothills and then we took a bus and finally, made dizzy by the hairpin bends devised in the last century by a brilliantly diabolical road-engineer, we alighted at the small hill station of Lansdowne, chief recruiting centre for the Garhwal Regiment.

Lansdowne is just over six thousand feet high. From there we walked, covering twenty-five miles between sunrise and sunset, until we came to Manjari village, clinging to the terraced slopes of a very proud, very permanent mountain.

And this is my fourth morning in the village.

Other mornings I was woken by the throaty chuckles of the red-billed blue magpies, as they glided between oak trees and medlars; but today the cicada has drowned all bird song. It is a little out of season for cicadas but perhaps this sudden warm spell in late September has deceived him into thinking it is mating season again.

Early though it is I am the last to get up. Gajadhar is exercising in the courtyard, going through an odd combination of Swedish exercises and yoga. He has a fine physique with the sturdy legs that most Garhwalis possess. I am sure he will realise his ambition of joining the Indian Army as a cadet. His younger brother Chakradhar, who is slim and fair with high cheek-bones, is milking the family's buffalo. Normally, he would be on his long walk to school, five miles distant; but this is a holiday, so he can stay at home and help with the household chores.

His mother is lighting a fire. She is a handsome woman, even though her ears, weighed down by heavy silver earrings, have lost their natural shape. Garhwali women usually invest their savings in silver ornaments. And at the time of marriage it is the boy's parents who make a gift of land to the parents of an attractive girl; a dowry system in reverse. There are fewer women than men in the hills and their good looks and sturdy physique give them considerable status among the men-folk.

Chakradhar's father is a corporal in the Indian Army and is away for most of the year.

When Gajadhar marries, his wife will stay in the village to help his mother and younger brother look after the fields, house, goats and buffalo. Gajadhar will see her only when he comes home on leave. He prefers it that way; he does not think a simple hill girl should be exposed to the sophisticated temptations of the plains.

The village is far above the river and most of the fields depend on rainfall. But water must be fetched for cooking, washing and drinking. And so, after a breakfast of hot sweet milk and thick *chapaties* stuffed with minced radish, the brothers and I set off down the rough track to the river.

The sun has climbed the mountains but it has yet to reach the narrow valley. We bathe in the river. Gajadhar and Chakradhar dive off a massive rock; but I wade in circumspectly, unfamiliar with the river's depths and currents. The water, a milky blue has come from the melting snows; it is very cold. I bathe quickly and then dash for a strip of sand where a little sunshine has split down the mountainside in warm, golden pools of light. At the same time the song of the whistling-thrush emerges like a dark secret from the wooded shadows.

A little later, buckets filled we toil up the steep mountain. We must go by a better path this time if we are not to come tumbling down with our buckets of water. As we climb we are mocked by a barbet which sits high up in a spruce calling feverishly in its monotonous mournful way.

We call it the mewli bird," says Gajadhar, "there is a story about it. People say that the souls of men who have suffered injuries in the law courts of the plains and who have died of their disappointments, transmigrate into the mewli birds. That is why the birds are always crying *un-nee-ow, un-nee-ow*, which means "injustice, injustice!"

The path leads us past a primary school, a small temple, and a single shop in which it is possible to buy salt, soap and a few other necessities. It is also the post office. And today it is serving as a lock-up.

The villagers have apprehended a local thief, who specialises in stealing jewellery from women while they are working in the fields. He is awaiting escort to the Lansdowne police station, and the shop-keeper-cum-postmaster-cum-constable brings him out for us to inspect. He is a mild-looking fellow, clearly shy of the small crowd that has gathered round him. I wonder how he manages to deprive the strong hill-women of their jewellery; it could not be by force! In any case crimes of violence are rare in Garhwal;

and robbery too, is uncommon for the simple reason that there is very little to rob.

The thief is rather glad of my presence, as it distracts attention from him. Strangers seldom come to Manjari. The crowd leaves him, turns to me, eager to catch a glimpse of the stranger in its midst. The children exclaim, point at me with delight, chatter among themselves. I might be a visitor from another planet instead of just an itinerant writer from the plains.

The postman has yet to arrive. The mail is brought in relays from Lansdowne. The Manjari postman who has to cover eight miles and delivers letters at several small villages on his route, should arrive around noon. He also serves as a newspaper, bringing the villagers news of the outside world. Over the years he has acquired a reputation for being highly inventive, sometimes creating his own news; so much so that when he told the villagers that men had landed on the moon, no one believed him. There are still a few sceptics.

Gajadhar has been walking out of the village every day, anxious to meet the postman. He is expecting a letter giving the results of his army entrance examination. If he is successful he will be called for an interview. And then, if he is accepted, he will be trained as an officer-cadet. After two years he will become a second lieutenant. His father, after twelve years in the army is still only a corporal. But his father never went to school. There were no schools in the hills during the father's youth.

The Manjari school is only up to Class five and it has about forty pupils. If these children (most of them boys) want to study any further, then, like Chakradhar, they must walk the five miles to the high school at the next big village.

"Don't you get tired walking ten miles every day?" I ask Chakradhar.

"I am used to it," he says. "I like walking."

I know that he only has two meals a day—one at seven in the morning when he leaves home and the other at six or seven in the evening when he returns from school—and I ask him if he does not get hungry on the way.

"There is always the wild fruit," he replies.

It appears that he is an expert on wild fruit: the purple berries of the thorny bilberry bushes ripening in May and June; wild strawberries like drops of blood on the dark green monsoon grass; small sour cherries and tough medlars in the winter months. Chakradhar's strong teeth and probing tongue extract whatever tang or sweetness lies hidden in them. And in March there are the rhododendron flowers. His mother makes them into jam. But Chakradhar likes them as they are: he places the petals on his tongue and chews till the sweet juice trickles down his throat.

He has never been ill.

"But what happens when someone is ill?" I ask knowing that in Manjari there are no medicines, no dispensary or hospital.

"He goes to bed until he is better," says Gajadhar. "We have a few home remedies. But if someone is very sick, we carry the person to the hospital at Lansdowne." He pauses as though wondering how much he should say, then shrugs and says: "Last year my uncle was very ill. He had a terrible pain in his stomach. For two days he cried out with the pain. So we made a litter and started out for Lansdowne. We had already carried him fifteen miles when he died. And then we had to carry him back again."

Some of the villages have dispensaries managed by compounders but the remoter areas of Garhwal are completely without medical aid. To the outsider, life in the Garhwal hills may seem idyllic and the people simple. But the Garhwali is far from being simple and his life is one long struggle, especially if he happens to be living in a high altitude village snowbound for four months in the year, with cultivation coming to a standstill and people having to manage with the food gathered and stored during the summer months.

Fortunately, the clear mountain air and the simple diet keep the Garhwalis free from most diseases, and help them recover from the more common ailments. The greatest dangers come from unexpected disasters, such as an accident with an axe or scythe, or an attack by a wild animal. A few years back, several Manjari children and old women were killed by a man-eating leopard. The leopard was finally killed by the villagers who hunted it down with spears and axes. But the leopard that sometimes prowls round the village at night looking for a stray dog or goat, slinks away at the approach of a human.

I do not see the leopard but at night I am woken by a rumbling and thumping on the roof. I wake Gajadhar and ask him what is happening.

"It is only a bear," he says.

"Is it trying to get in?"

"No, It's been in the cornfield and now it's after the pumpkins on the roof."

A little later, when we look out of the small window, we see a black bear making off like a thief in the night, a large pumpkin held securely to his chest.

At the approach of winter when snow covers the higher mountains the brown and black Himalayan bears descend to lower altitudes in search of food. Because they are short-sighted and suspicious of anything that moves, they can be dangerous; but, like most wild animals, they will avoid men if they can and are aggressive only when accompanied by their cubs.

Gajadhar advises me to run downhill if chased by a bear. He says that bears find it easier to run uphill than downhill.

I am not interested in being chased by a bear, but the following night Gajadhar and I stay up to try and prevent the bear from depleting his cornfield. We take up our position on a highway promontory of rock, which gives us a clear view of the moonlit field.

A little after midnight, the bear comes down to the edge of the field but he is suspicious and has probably smelt us. He is, however, hungry; and so, after standing up as high as possible on his hind legs and peering about to see if the field is empty, he comes cautiously out of the forest and makes his way towards the corn.

When about half-way, his attention is suddenly attracted by some Buddhist prayer-flags which have been strung up recently between two small trees by a band of wandering Tibetans. On spotting the flags the bear gives a little grunt of disapproval and begins to move back into the forest; but the fluttering of the little flags is a puzzle that he feels he must make out (for a bear is one of the most inquisitive animals); so after a few backward steps, he again stops and watches them.

Not satisfied with this, he stands on his hind legs looking at the flags, first at one side and then at the other. Then seeing that they do not attack him and so not appear dangerous, he makes his way right up to the flags taking only two or three steps at a time and having a good look before each advance. Eventually, he moves confidently up to the flags and pulls them all down. Then, after careful examination of the flags, he moves into the field of corn.

But Gajadhar has decided that he is not going to lose any more corn, so he starts shouting, and the rest of the village wakes up and people come out of their houses beating drums and empty kerosene tins.

Deprived of his dinner, the bear makes off in a bad temper. He runs downhill and at a good speed too; and I am glad that I am not in his path just then. Uphill or downhill an angry bear is best given a very wide berth.

For Gajadhar, impatient to know the result of his army entrance examination, the following day is a trial of his patience.

First, we hear that there has been a landslide and that the postman cannot reach us. Then, we hear that although there has been a landslide, the postman has already passed the spot in safety. Another alarming rumour has it that the postman disappeared with the landslide. This is soon denied. The postman is safe. It was only the mail-bag that disappeared.

And then, at two in the afternoon, the postman turns up. He tells us that there was indeed a landslide but that it took place on someone else's route. Apparently, a mischievous urchin who passed him on the way was responsible for all the rumours. But we suspect the postman of having something to do with them....

Gajadhar had passed his examination and will leave with me in the morning. We have to be up early in order to reach Lansdowne before dark. But Gajadhar's mother insists on celebrating her son's success by feasting her friends and neighbours. There is a partridge (a present from a neighbour who had decided that Gajadhar will make a fine husband for his daughter), and two chickens: rich fare for folk whose normal diet consists mostly of lentils, potatoes and onions.

After dinner, there are songs, and Gajadhar's mother sings of the homesickness of those who are separated from their loved ones and their home in the hills. It is an old Garhwali folk-song:

Oh, mountain-swift, you are from my father's home;
Speak, oh speak, in the courtyard of my parents,
My mother will hear you; She will send my brother to
fetch me.

A grain of rice alone in the cooking pot
Cries, "I wish I could get out!"
Likewise I wonder:
"Will I ever reach my father's house?"

The *hookah* is passed round and stories are told. Tales of ghosts and demons mingle with legends of ancient kings and heroes. It is almost midnight by the time the last guest has gone. Chakradhar approaches me as I am about to retire for the night.

"Will you come again?" he asks.

"Yes, I'll come again," I reply. "If not next year, then the year after. How many years are left before you finish school?"

"Four".

"Four years. If you walk ten miles a day for four years, how many miles will that make?"

"Four thousand and six hundred miles," says Chakradhar after a moment's thought, "but we have two month's holiday each year. That means I'll walk about twelve thousand miles in four years."

The moon has not yet risen. Lanterns swing in the dark.

The lanterns flit silently over the hillside and go out one by one. This Garhwali day, which is just like any other day in the hills, slips quietly into the silence of the mountains.

I stretch myself out on my cot. Outside the small window the sky is brilliant with stars. As I close my eyes, someone brushes against the lime tree, brushing its leaves; and the fresh fragrance of limes comes to me on the night air, making the moment memorable for all time.

Haikus and Other Short Verses

Whenever I am in a pensive or troubled state of mind, I read (or write) a Haiku. It helps to clear and calm my mind. Here are a few that I wrote last year...

Sweet-scented jasmine in this fold of cloth,
I give to you on this your bridal day,
That you forget me not.

※

There's a begonia in her cheeks,
Pink as the flush of early dawn
On Sikkim's peaks.

※

Her beauty brought her fame
But only the wild rose flowering beside her grave
Is there to hear her whispered name:
Gulabi.

*

Bright red
The poinsettia flames
As autumn and the old year wanes.

*

Petunias I will praise,
Their soft perfume
Takes me by surprise!

*

The Indian Pink keeps flowering without end,
Sturdy and modest,
A loyal friend.

*

Shaded in a deep ravine,
The ferns stand upright, dark and green.

*

One fine day my kite took wing,
Then came a strong wind—
I was left with the string.

*

To the temple on the mountain top
We climbed. Forgot to pray!
But got home anyway.

※

Antirrhinums line the wall,
Sturdy little dragons all!

※

While I was yet a boy, I dreamt of power and fame;
And now I'm old, I dream of being a boy again.

※

Spider running up the wall
Means that rain is going to fall.

※

Spider running down the wall
Means the house is going to fall!

※

Jasmine flowers in her hair,
Languid summer days are here,
And sweet longing scents the air.

A Long Walk for Bina

1

A Leopard, lithe and sinewy, drank at the mountain stream, and then lay down on the grass to bask in the late February sunshine. Its tail twitched occasionally and the animal appeared to be sleeping. At the sound of distant voices it raised its head to listen, then stood up and leapt lightly over the boulders in the stream, disappearing among the trees on the opposite bank.

A minute or two later, three children came walking down the forest path. They were a girl and two boys, and they were singing in their local dialect an old song they had learnt from their grandparents.

Five more miles to go!
We climb through rain and snow.

A river to cross...
a mountain to pass...
Now we've four more miles to go!

Their school satchels looked new, their clothes had been washed and pressed. Their loud and cheerful singing startled a Spotted Forktail. The bird left its favourite rock in the stream and flew down the dark ravine.

'Well, we have only three more miles to go,' said the bigger boy, Prakash, who had been this way hundreds of times. 'But first we have to cross the stream.'

He was a sturdy twelve-year-old with eyes like blackcurrants and a mop of bushy hair that refused to settle down on his head. The girl and her small brother were taking this path for the first time.

'I'm feeling tired, Bina,' said the little boy.

Bina smiled at him, and Prakash said, 'Don't worry, Sonu, you'll get used to the walk. There's plenty of time.' He glanced at the old watch he'd been given by his grandfather. It needed constant winding. 'We can rest here for five or six minutes.'

They sat down on a smooth boulder and watched the clear water of the shallow stream tumbling downhill. Bina examined the old watch on Prakash's wrist. The glass was badly scratched and she could barely make out the figures on the dial. 'Are you sure it still gives the right time?' she asked.

'Well, it loses five minutes every day, so I put it ten minutes forward at night. That means by morning it's quite accurate! Even our teacher, Mr. Mani, asks me for the time. If he doesn't ask, I tell him! The clock in our classroom keeps stopping.'

They removed their shoes and let the cold mountain water run over their feet. Bina was the same age as Prakash. She had pink cheeks, soft brown eyes, and hair that was just beginning to lose its natural curls. Hers was a gentle face, but a determined little chin showed that she could be a strong person. Sonu, her younger brother, was ten. He was a thin boy who had been sickly as a child but was now beginning to fill out. Although he did not look very athletic, he could run like the wind.

Bina had been going to school in her own village of Koli, on the other side of the mountain. But it had been a Primary School, finishing at Class Five. Now, in order to study in the Sixth, she would have to walk several miles every day to Nauti, where there was a High School going up to the Eighth. It had been decided that Sonu would also shift to the new school, to give Bina company. Prakash, their neighbour in Koli, was already a pupil at the Nauti school. His mischievous nature, which sometimes got him into trouble, had resulted in his having to repeat a year.

But this didn't seem to bother him. 'What's the hurry?' he had told his indignant parents. 'You're not sending me to a foreign land when I finish school. And our cows aren't running away, are they?'

'You would prefer to look after the cows, wouldn't you?' asked Bina, as they got up to continue their walk.

'Oh, school's all right. Wait till you see old Mr. Mani. He always gets our names mixed up, as well as the subjects he's supposed to be teaching. At our last lesson, instead of maths, he gave us a geography lesson!'

'More fun than maths,' said Bina.

'Yes, but there's a new teacher this year. She's very young they say, just out of college. I wonder what she'll be like.'

Bina walked faster and Sonu had some trouble keeping up with them. She was excited about the new school and the prospect of different surroundings. She had seldom been outside her own village, with its small school and single ration shop. The day's routine never varied—helping her mother in the fields or with household tasks like fetching water from the spring or cutting grass and fodder for the cattle. Her father, who was a soldier, was away for nine months in the year and Sonu was still too small for the heavier tasks.

As they neared Nauti village, they were joined by other children coming from different directions. Even where there were no major roads, the mountains were full of little lanes and short cuts. Like a game of snakes and ladders, these narrow paths zigzagged around the hills and villages, cutting through fields and crossing narrow ravines until they came together to form a fairly busy road along which mules, cattle and goats joined the throng.

Nauti was a fairly large village, and from here a broader but dustier road started for Tehri. There was a small bus, several trucks and (for part of the way) a road-roller. The road hadn't been completed because the heavy diesel roller couldn't take the steep climb to Nauti. It stood on the roadside half way up the road from Tehri.

Prakash knew almost everyone in the area, and exchanged greetings and gossip with other children as well as with muleteers, bus-drivers, milkmen and labourers working on the road. He loved telling everyone the time, even if they weren't interested.

'It's nine o'clock,' he would announce, glancing at his wrist. 'Isn't your bus leaving today?'

'Off with you!' the bus-driver would respond, 'I'll leave when I'm ready.'

As the children approached Nauti, the small flat school buildings came into view on the outskirts of the village, fringed with a line of long-leaved pines. A small crowd had assembled on the one playing field. Something unusual seemed to have happened. Prakash ran forward to see what it was all about. Bina and Sonu stood aside, waiting in a patch of sunlight near the boundary wall.

Prakash soon came running back to them. He was bubbling over with excitement.

'It's Mr. Mani!' he gasped. 'He's disappeared! People are saying a leopard must have carried him off!'

2

Mr. Mani wasn't really old. He was about fifty-five and was expected to retire soon. But for the children, most adults over forty seemed ancient! And Mr. Mani had always been a bit absent-minded, even as a young man.

He had gone out for his early morning walk, saying he'd be back by eight o'clock, in time to have his breakfast and be ready for class. He wasn't married, but his sister and her husband stayed with him. When it was past nine o'clock his sister presumed he'd stopped at a neighbour's house for breakfast (he loved tucking into other people's breakfast) and that he had gone on to school from there. But when the school bell rang at ten o'clock, and everyone but Mr. Mani was present, questions were asked and guesses were made.

No one had seen him return from his walk and enquiries made in the village showed that he had not stopped at anyone's house. For Mr. Mani to disappear was puzzling; for him to disappear without his breakfast was extraordinary.

Then a milkman returning from the next village said he had seen a leopard sitting on a rock on the outskirts of the pine forest. There had been talk of a cattle-killer in the valley, of leopard and other animals being displaced by the construction of a dam. But as yet no one had heard of a leopard attacking a man. Could Mr. Mani have been its first victim? Someone found a strip of red cloth entangled in a blackberry bush and went running through the village showing it to everyone. Mr. Mani had been known to wear red pyjamas. Surely, he had been seized and eaten! But where were his remains? And why had he been in his pyjamas?

Meanwhile, Bina and Sonu and the rest of the children had followed their teachers into the school playground. Feeling a little lost, Bina looked around for Prakash. She found herself facing a dark slender young woman wearing spectacles, who must have been in her early twenties—just a little too old to be another student. She had a kind expressive face and she seemed a little concerned by all that had been happening.

Bina noticed that she had lovely hands; it was obvious that the new teacher hadn't milked cows or worked in the fields!

'You must be new here,' said the teacher, smiling at Bina. 'And is this your little brother?'

'Yes, we've come from Koli village. We were at school there.'

'It's a long walk from Koli. You didn't see any leopards, did you? Well, I'm new too. Are you in the Sixth class?'

'Sonu is in the Third. I'm in the Sixth.'

'Then I'm your new teacher. My name is Tania Ramola. Come along, let's see if we can settle down in our classroom.'

Mr. Mani turned up at twelve o'clock, wondering what all the fuss was about. No, he snapped, he had not been attacked by a leopard; and yes, he had lost his pyjamas and would someone kindly return them to him?

'How did you lose your pyjamas, Sir?' asked Prakash.

'They were blown off the washing line!' snapped Mr. Mani.

After much questioning, Mr. Mani admitted that he had

gone further than he had intended, and that he had lost his way coming back. He had been a bit upset because the new teacher, a slip of a girl, had been given charge of the Sixth, while he was still with the Fifth, along with that troublesome boy Prakash, who kept on reminding him of the time! The Headmaster had explained that as Mr. Mani was due to retire at the end of the year, the school did not wish to burden him with a senior class. But Mr. Mani looked upon the whole thing as a plot to get rid of him. He glowered at Miss Ramola whenever he passed her. And when she smiled back at him, he looked the other way!

Mr. Mani had been getting even more absent-minded of late—putting on his shoes without his socks, wearing his homespun waistcoat inside out, mixing up people's names, and of course, eating other people's lunches and dinners. His sister had made a mutton broth for the postmaster, who was down with 'flu' and had asked Mr. Mani to take it over in a thermos. When the postmaster opened the thermos, he found only a few drops of broth at the bottom—Mr. Mani had drunk the rest somewhere along the way.

When sometimes Mr. Mani spoke of his coming retirement, it was to describe his plans for the small field he owned just behind the house. Right now, it was full of potatoes, which did not require much looking after; but he had plans for growing dahlias, roses, French beans, and other fruits and flowers.

The next time he visited Tehri, he promised himself, he would buy some dahlia bulbs and rose cuttings. The monsoon season would be a good time to put them down. And meanwhile, his potatoes were still flourishing.

3

Bina enjoyed her first day at the new school. She felt at ease with Miss Ramola, as did most of the boys and girls in her class. Tania Ramola had been to distant towns such as Delhi and Lucknow—places they had only heard about—and it was said that she had a brother who was a pilot and flew planes all over the world. Perhaps he'd fly over Nauti some day!

Most of the children had of course, seen planes flying overhead, but none of them had seen a ship, and only a few had been in a train. Tehri mountain was far from the railway and hundreds of miles from the sea. But they all knew about the big dam that was being built at Tehri, just forty miles away.

Bina, Sonu and Prakash had company for part of the way home, but gradually the other children went off in different directions. Once they had crossed the stream, they were on their own again.

It was a steep climb all the way back to their village. Prakash had a supply of peanuts which he shared with Bina and Sonu, and at a small spring they quenched their thirst.

When they were less than a mile from home, they met a postman who had finished his round of the villages in the area and was now returning to Nauti.

'Don't waste time along the way,' he told them. 'Try to get home before dark.'

'What's the hurry?' asked Prakash, glancing at his watch. 'It's only five o'clock.'

'There's a leopard around. I saw it this morning, not far from the stream. No one is sure how it got here. So don't take any chances. Get home early.'

'So there really is a leopard,' said Sonu.

They took his advice and walked faster, and Sonu forgot to complain about his aching feet.

They were home well before sunset.

There was a smell of cooking in the air and they were hungry.

'Cabbage and roti,' said Prakash gloomily. 'But I could eat anything today.' He stopped outside his small slate-roofed house, and Bina and Sonu waved good-bye and carried on across a couple of ploughed fields until they reached their small stone house.

'Stuffed tomatoes,' said Sonu, sniffing just outside the front door.

'And lemon pickle,' said Bina, who had helped cut, sun and salt the lemons a month previously.

Their mother was lighting the kitchen stove. They greeted her with great hugs and demands for an immediate dinner. She was a good cook who could make even the simplest of dishes taste delicious. Her favourite saying was, 'Home-made bread is better than roast meat abroad,' and Bina and Sonu had to agree.

Electricity had yet to reach their village, and they took their meal by the light of a kerosene lamp. After the meal,

Sonu settled down to do a little homework, while Bina stepped outside to look at the stars.

Across the fields, someone was playing a flute. 'It must be Prakash,' thought Bina. 'He always breaks off on the high notes.' But the flute music was simple and appealing, and she began singing softly to herself in the dark.

4

Mr. Mani was having trouble with the porcupines. They had been getting into his garden at night and digging up and eating his potatoes. From his bedroom window—left open, now that the mild-April weather had arrived—he could listen to them enjoying the vegetables he had worked hard to grow. Srunch, scrunch! *Katar, katar*, as their sharp teeth sliced through the largest and juiciest of potatoes. For Mr. Mani it was as though they were biting through his own flesh. And the sound of them digging industriously as they rooted up those healthy, leafy plants, made him tremble with rage and indignation. The unfairness of it all!

Yes, Mr. Mani hated porcupines. He prayed for their destruction, their removal from the face of the earth. But, as his friends were quick to point out, 'The creator made porcupines too,' and in any case you could never see the creatures or catch them, they were completely nocturnal.

Mr. Mani got out of bed every night, torch in one hand, a stout stick in the other, but as soon as he stepped into the garden the crunching and digging stopped and he was greeted by the most infuriating of silences. He would grope around in the dark, swinging wildly with the stick, but not a single porcupine was to be seen or heard. As soon as he was back in bed—the sounds would start all over again. Scrunch, scrunch, *katar, katar*....

Mr. Mani came to his class tired and dishevelled, with rings beneath his eyes and a permanent frown on his face. It took some time for his pupils to discover the reason for his misery, but when they did, they felt sorry for their teacher and took to discussing ways and means of saving his potatoes from the porcupines.

It was Prakash who came up with the idea of a moat or waterditch. 'Porcupines don't like water,' he said knowledgeably.

'How do you know?' asked one of his friends.

'Throw water on one and see how it runs! They don't like getting their quills wet.'

There was no one who could disprove Prakash's theory, and the class fell in with the idea of building a moat, especially as it meant getting most of the day off.

'Anything to make Mr. Mani happy,' said the Headmaster, and the rest of the school watched with envy as the pupils of Class Five, armed with spades and shovels collected from all parts of the village, took up their positions around Mr. Mani's potato field and begun digging a ditch.

By evening the moat was ready, but it was still dry and the porcupines got in again that night and had a great feast.

'At this rate,' said Mr. Mani gloomily, 'there won't be any potatoes left to save.'

But next day Prakash and the other boys and girls managed to divert the water from a stream that flowed past the village. They had the satisfaction of watching it flow gently into the ditch. Everyone went home in a good mood. By nightfall, the ditch had overflowed, the potato field was flooded, and Mr. Mani found himself trapped inside his house. But Prakash and his friends had won the day. The porcupines stayed away that night!

A month had passed, and wild violets, daisies and buttercups now sprinkled the hill slopes, and on her way to school Bina gathered enough to make a little posy. The bunch of flowers fitted easily into an old ink-well. Miss Ramola was delighted to find this little display in the middle of her desk.

'Who put these here?' she asked in surprise.

Bina kept quiet, and the rest of the class smiled secretively. After that, they took turns bringing flowers for the classroom.

On her long walks to school and home again, Bina became aware that April was the month of new leaves. The oak leaves were bright green above and silver beneath, and when they rippled in the breeze they were clouds of silvery green. The path was strewn with old leaves, dry and crackly. Sonu loved kicking them around.

Clouds of white butterflies floated across the stream. Sonu was chasing a butterfly when he stumbled over something dark and repulsive. He went sprawling on the grass. When he got to his feet, he looked down at the remains of a small animal.

'Bina! Prakash! Come quickly!' he shouted.

It was part of a sheep, killed some days earlier by a much larger animal.

'Only a leopard could have done this,' said Prakash.

'Let's get away, then,' said Sonu. 'It might still be around!'

'No, there's nothing left to eat. The leopard will be hunting elsewhere by now. Perhaps it's moved on to the next valley.'

'Still, I'm frightened,' said Sonu. 'There may be more leopards!'

Bina took him by the hand. 'Leopards don't attack humans!' she said.

'They will, if they get a taste for people!' insisted Prakash.

'Well, this one hasn't attacked any people as yet,' said Bina, although she couldn't be sure. Hadn't there been rumours of a leopard attacking some workers near the dam? But she did not want Sonu to feel afraid, so she did not mention the story. All she said was, 'It has probably come here because of all the activity near the dam.'

All the same, they hurried home. And for a few days, whenever they reached the stream, they crossed over very quickly, unwilling to linger too long at that lovely spot.

5

A few days later, a school party was on its way to Tehri to see the new dam that was being built.

Miss Ramola had arranged to take her class, and Mr. Mani, not wishing to be left out, insisted on taking his class as well.

That meant there were about fifty boys and girls taking part in the outing. The little bus could only take thirty. A friendly truck-driver agreed to take some children if they were prepared to sit on sacks of potatoes. And Prakash persuaded the owner of the diesel-roller to turn it round and head it back to Tehri—with him and a couple of friends up on the driving seat.

Prakash's small group set off at sunrise, as they had to walk some distance in order to reach the stranded road-roller. The bus left at 9 a.m. with Miss Ramola and her class, and Mr. Mani and some of his pupils. The truck was to follow later.

It was Bina's first visit to a large town, and her first bus ride.

The sharp curves along the winding, downhill road made several children feel sick. The bus-driver seemed to be in a tearing hurry. He took them along at rolling, rollicking speed, which made Bina feel quite giddy. She rested her head on her arms and refused to look out of the window. Hairpin bends and cliff edges, pine forests and snowcapped peaks, all swept past her, but she felt too ill to want to look at anything. It was just as well—those sudden drops, hundreds of feet to the valley below, were quite frightening. Bina began to wish that she hadn't come—or that she had joined Prakash on the road-roller instead!

Miss Ramola and Mr. Mani didn't seem to notice the lurching and groaning of the old bus. They had made this journey many times. They were busy arguing about the advantages and disadvantages of large dams—an argument that was to continue on and off for much of the day.

Meanwhile, Prakash and his friends had reached the roller. The driver hadn't turned up, but they managed to reverse it and get it going in the direction of Tehri. They were soon overtaken by both bus and truck but kept moving along at a steady chug. Prakash spotted Bina at the window of the bus and waved cheerfully. She responded feebly.

Bina felt better when the road levelled out near Tehri. As they crossed an old bridge over the wide river, they were startled by a loud bang which made the bus shudder. A cloud of dust rose above the town.

'They're blasting the mountain,' said Miss Ramola.

'End of a mountain,' said Mr. Mani, mournfully.

While they were drinking cups of tea at the bus stop, waiting for the potato truck and the road-roller, Miss Ramola and Mr. Mani continued their argument about the dam. Miss Ramola maintained that it would bring electric power and water for irrigation to large areas of the country, including the surrounding area. Mr. Mani declared that it was a menace, as it was situated in an earthquake zone. There would be a terrible disaster if the dam burst! Bina found it all very confusing. And what about the animals in the area, she wondered, what would happen to them?

The argument was becoming quite heated when the potato truck arrived. There was no sign of the road-roller, so it was decided that Mr. Mani should wait for Prakash and his friends while Miss Ramola's group went ahead.

Some eight or nine miles before Tehri the road-roller had broken down, and Prakash and his friends were forced to walk. They had not gone far, however, when a mule train came along—five or six mules that had been delivering sacks of grain in Nauti. A boy rode on the first mule, but the others had no loads.

'Can you give us a ride to Tehri?' called Prakash.

'Make yourselves comfortable,' said the boy.

There were no saddles, only gunny sacks strapped on to the mules with rope. They had a rough but jolly ride down to the Tehri bus stop. None of them had ever ridden mules; but they had saved at least an hour on the road.

Looking around the bus stop for the rest of the party, they could find no one from their school. And Mr. Mani, who should have been waiting for them, had vanished.

6

Tania Ramola and her group had taken the steep road to the hill above Tehri. Half an hour's climbing brought them to a little plateau which overlooked the town, the river and the dam-site.

The earthworks for the dam were only just coming up, but a wide tunnel had been bored through the mountain to divert the river into another channel. Down below the old town was still spread out across the valley and from a distance it looked quite charming and picturesque.

'Will the whole town be swallowed up by the waters of the dam?' asked Bina.

'Yes, all of it,' said Miss Ramola. 'The clock tower and the old palace. The long bazaar, and the temples, the schools and the jail, and hundreds of houses, for many miles up the valley. All those people will have to go—thousands of them! Of course, they'll be resettled elsewhere.'

'But the town's been here for hundreds of years,' said Bina. 'They were quite happy without the dam, weren't they?'

'I suppose they were. But the dam isn't just for them—it's for the millions who live further downstream, across the plains.'

'And it doesn't matter what happens to this place?'

'The local people will be given new homes, somewhere else.' Miss Ramola found herself on the defensive and decided to change the subject. 'Everyone must be hungry. It's time we had our lunch.'

Bina kept quiet. She didn't think the local people would want to go away. And it was a good thing, she mused, that there was only a small stream and not a big river running past her village. To be uprooted like this—a town and hundreds of villages—and put down somewhere on the hot, dusty plains—seemed to her unbearable.

'Well, I'm glad I don't live in Tehri,' she said.

She did not know it, but all the animals and most of the birds had already left the area. The leopard had been among them.

They walked through the colourful, crowded bazaar, where fruit-sellers did business beside silversmiths, and pavement vendors sold everything from umbrellas to glass bangles. Sparrows attacked sacks of grain, monkeys made off with bananas, and stray cows and dogs rummaged in refuse bins, but nobody took any notice. Music blarred from radios. Buses blew their horns. Sonu bought a whistle to add to the general din, but Miss Ramola told him to put it away. Bina had kept five rupees aside, and now she used it to buy a cotton head-scarf for her mother.

As they were about to enter a small restaurant for a meal, they were joined by Prakash and his companions; but of Mr. Mani there was still no sign.

'He must have met one of his relatives,' said Prakash. 'He has relatives everywhere.'

After a simple meal of rice and lentils, they walked the length of the bazaar without seeing Mr. Mani. At last, when they were about to give up the search, they saw him emerge from a by-lane, a large sack slung over his shoulder.

'Sir, where have you been?' asked Prakash. 'We have been looking for you everywhere.'

On Mr. Mani's face was a look of triumph.

'Help me with this bag,' he said breathlessly.

'You've bought more potatoes, sir,' said Prakash.

'Not potatoes, boy. Dahlia bulbs!'

7

It was dark by the time they were all back in Nauti. Mr. Mani had refused to be separated from his sack of dahlia bulbs, and had been forced to sit in the back of the truck with Prakash and most of the boys.

Bina did not feel so ill on the return journey. Going uphill was definitely better than going downhill! But by the time the bus reached Nauti it was too late for most of the children to walk back to the more distant villages. The boys were put up in different homes, while the girls were given beds in the school verandah.

The night was warm and still. Large moths fluttered around the single bulb that lit the verandah. Counting moths, Sonu soon fell asleep. But Bina stayed awake for some time, listening to the sounds of the night. A nightjar went *tonk-tonk* in the bushes, and somewhere in the forest an owl hooted softly. The sharp call of a barking-deer travelled up the valley, from the direction of the stream. Jackals kept howling. It seemed that there were more of them than ever before.

Bina was not the only one to hear the barking-deer. The leopard, stretched full length on a rocky ledge, heard it too. The leopard raised its head and then got up slowly. The deer was its natural prey. But there weren't many left, and that was why the leopard, robbed of its forest by the dam, had taken to attacking dogs and cattle near the villages.

As the cry of the barking-deer sounded nearer, the leopard left its look-out point and moved swiftly through the shadows towards the stream.

8

In early June the hills were dry and dusty, and forest fires broke out, destroying shrubs and trees, killing birds and small animals. The resin in the pines made these trees burn more fiercely, and the wind would take sparks from the trees and carry them into the dry grass and leaves, so that new fires would spring up before the old ones had died out. Fortunately, Bina's village was not in the pine belt; the fires did not reach it. But Nauti was surrounded by a fire that raged for three days, and the children had to stay away from school.

And then, towards the end of June, the monsoon rains arrived and there was an end to forest fires. The monsoon lasts three months and the lower Himalayas could be drenched in rain, mist and cloud for the next three months.

The first rain arrived while Bina, Prakash and Sonu were returning home from school. Those first few drops on the dusty path made them cry out with excitement. Then the rain grew heavier and a wonderful aroma rose from the earth.

'The best smell in the world!' exclaimed Bina.

Everything suddenly came to life. The grass, the crops, the trees, the birds. Even the leaves of the trees glistened and looked new.

That first wet weekend, Bina and Sonu helped their mother plant beans, maize and cucumbers. Sometimes, when the rain was very heavy, they had to run indoors.

Otherwise they worked in the rain, the soft mud clinging to their bare legs.

Prakash now owned a dog, a black dog with one ear up and one ear down. The dog ran around getting in everyone's way, barking at cows, goats, hens and humans, without frightening any of them. Prakash said it was a very clever dog, but not one else seemed to think so. Prakash also said it would protect the village from the leopard, but others said the dog would be the first to be taken—he'd run straight into the jaws of Mr. Spots!

In Nauti, Tania Ramola was trying to find a dry spot in the quarters she'd been given. It was an old building and the roof was leaking in several places. Mugs and buckets were scattered about the floor in order to catch the drip.

Mr. Mani had dug up all his potatoes and presented them to the friends and neighbours who had given him lunches and dinners. He was having the time of his life, planting dahlia bulbs all over his garden.

'I'll have a field of many-coloured dahlias!' he announced. 'Just wait till the end of August!'

'Watch out for those porcupines,' warned his sister. 'They eat dahlia bulbs too!'

Mr. Mani made an inspection tour of his moat, no longer in flood, and found everything in good order. Prakash had done his job well.

Now, when the children crossed the stream, they found that the water-level had risen by about a foot. Small cascades had turned into water-falls. Ferns had sprung up on the banks. Frogs chanted.

Prakash and his dog dashed across the stream. Bina and Sonu followed more cautiously. The current was much stronger now and the water was almost up to their knees. Once they had crossed the stream, they hurried along the path, anxious not to be caught in a sudden downpour.

By the time they reached school, each of them had two or three leeches clinging to their legs. They had to use salt to remove them. The leeches were the most troublesome part of the rainy season. Even the leopard did not like them. It could not lie in the long grass without getting leeches on its paws and face.

One day, when Bina, Prakash and Sonu were about to cross the stream they heard a low rumble, which grew louder every second. Looking up at the opposite hill, they saw several trees shudder, tilt outwards and begin to fall. Earth and rocks bulged out from the mountain, then came crashing down into the ravine.

'Landslide!' shouted Sonu.

'It's carried away the path,' said Bina. 'Don't go any further.'

There was a tremendous roar as more rocks, trees and bushes fell away and crashed down the hillside.

Prakash's dog, who had gone ahead, came running back, tail between his legs.

They remained rooted to the spot until the rocks had stopped falling and the dust had settled. Birds circled the area, calling wildly. A frightened barking-deer ran past them.

'We can't go to school now,' said Prakash. 'There's no way around.'

They turned and trudged home through the gathering mist.

In Koli, Prakash's parents had heard the roar of the landslide. They were setting out in search of the children when they saw them emerge from the mist, waving cheerfully.

9

They had to miss school for another three days, and Bina was afraid they might not be able to take their final exams. Although Prakash was not really troubled at the thought of missing exams, he did not like feeling helpless just because their path had been swept away. So he explored the hillside until he found a goat-track going around the mountain. It joined up with another path near Nauti. This made their walk longer by a mile, but Bina did not mind. It was much cooler now that the rains were in full swing.

The only trouble with the new route was that it passed close to the leopard's lair. The animal had made this area its own since being forced to leave the dam area.

One day Prakash's dog ran ahead of them, barking furiously. Then he ran back, whimpering.

'He's always running away from something,' observed Sonu. But a minute later he understood the reason for the dog's fear.

They rounded a bend and Sonu saw the leopard standing in their way. They were struck dumb—too terrified to run. It was a strong, sinewy creature. A low growl rose from its throat. It seemed ready to spring.

They stood perfectly still, afraid to move or say a word. And the leopard must have been equally surprised. It stared at them for a few seconds, then bounded across the path and into the oak forest.

Sonu was shaking. Bina could hear her heart hammering. Prakash could only stammer: 'Did you see the way he sprang? Wasn't he beautiful?'

He forgot to look at his watch for the rest of the day.

A few days later Sonu stopped and pointed to a large outcrop of rock on the next hill.

The leopard stood far above them, outlined against the sky. It looked strong, majestic. Standing beside it were two young cubs.

'Look at those little ones!' exclaimed Sonu.

'So it's a female, not a male,' said Prakash.

'That's why she was killing so often,' said Bina. 'She had to feed her cubs too.'

They remained still for several minutes, gazing up at the leopard and her cubs. The leopard family took no notice of them.

'She knows we are here,' said Prakash, 'but she doesn't care. She knows we won't harm them.'

'We are cubs too!' said Sonu.

'Yes,' said Bina. 'And there's still plenty of space for all of us. Even when the dam is ready there will still be room for leopards and humans.'

10

The school exams were over. The rains were nearly over too. The landslide had been cleared, and Bina, Prakash and Sonu were once again crossing the stream.

There was a chill in the air, for it was the end of September.

Prakash had learnt to play the flute quite well, and he played on the way to school and then again on the way home. As a result he did not look at his watch so often.

One morning they found a small crowd in front of Mr. Mani's house.

'What could have happened?' wondered Bina. 'I hope he hasn't got lost again.'

'Maybe he's sick,' said Sonu.

'Maybe it's the porcupines,' said Prakash.

But it was none of these things.

Mr. Mani's first dahlia was in bloom, and half the village had turned out to look at it! It was a huge red double dahlia, so heavy that it had to be supported with sticks. No one had ever seen such a magnificent flower!

Mr. Mani was a happy man. And his mood only improved over the coming week, as more and more dahlias flowered—

crimson, yellow, purple, mauve, white—button dahlias, pom-pom dahlias, spotted dahlias, striped dahlias ... Mr. Mani had them all! A dahlia even turned up on Tania Romola's desk—he got quite well with her now—and another brightened up the Headmaster's study.

A week later, on their way home—it was almost the last day of the school term—Bina, Prakash and Sonu talked about what they might do when they grew up.

'I think I'll become a teacher,' said Bina. 'I'll teach children about animals and birds, and trees and flowers.'

'Better than maths!' said Prakash.

'I'll be a pilot,' said Sonu. 'I want to fly a plane like Miss Ramola's brother.'

'And what about you Prakash?' asked Bina.

Prakash just smiled and said, 'Maybe I'll be a flute-player,' and he put the flute to his lips and played a sweet melody.

'Well, the world needs flute-players too,' said Bina, as they fell into step beside him.

The leopard had been stalking a barking-deer. She paused when she heard the flute and the voices of the children. Her own young ones were growing quickly, but the girl and the two boys did not look much older.

They had started singing their favourite song again.

Five more miles to go!
We climb through rain and snow,
A river to cross—

A mountain to pass—
Now we've four more miles to go!

The leopard waited until they had passed, before returning to the trail of the barking-deer.

These Simple Things

The simplest things in life are best—
A patch of green,
A small bird's nest,
A drink of water, fresh and cold,
The taste of bread,
A song of old;
These are the things that matter most.
The laughter of a child,
A favourite book,
Flowers growing wild,
A cricket singing in a shady nook.
A ball that bounces high!
A summer shower,
A rainbow in the sky,

The touch of a loving hand,
And time to rest—
These simple things in life are best.

Mussoorie's Landour Bazaar

As in most north Indian bazaars, here too there is a clock tower. And, like most clocks in clock towers, this one works in fits and starts; listless in summer, sluggish during the monsoon, stopping altogether when it snows in January. Almost every year the tall brick structure gets a coat of paint. It was pink last year. Now it's a livid purple.

From the clock tower at one end to the mule sheds at the other, this old Mussoorie bazaar is a mile long. The tall, shaky three-storey buildings cling to the mountainside, shutting out the sunlight. They are even shakier now that heavy trucks have started rumbling down the narrow street, originally made for nothing heavier than a rickshaw. The street is narrow and damp, retaining all the bazaar smells; sweetmeats frying, smoke from wood or charcoal fires, the sweat and urine of mules, petrol fumes, all of which mingle with the smell of mist and old building and distant pines.

The bazaar sprang up about 150 years ago to serve the needs of British soldiers who were sent to the Landour convalescent depot to recover from sickness or wounds. The old military hospital, built in 1827, now houses the Defence Institute of Management.

The Landour Bazaar today serves the local population. There are a number of silversmiths in Landour. They fashion silver nose-rings, ear-rings, bracelets and anklets, which are bought by the women from the surrounding Jaunpuri village. One silversmith had a chestfull of old silver rupees. These rupees are sometimes hung on thin silver chains and worn as pendants.

At the other extreme there are the *kabari* shops, where you can pick up almost anything—a taperecorder discarded by a Woodstock student, or a piece of furniture from grandmother's time in the hill-station. Old clothes, Victorian bric-a-brac, and bits of modern gadgetry vie for your attention.

The old clothes are often more reliable than the new. Last winter I bought a pullover marked 'Made in Nepal' from a Tibetan pavement vendor. I was wearing it on the way home when it began to rain. By the time I reached my cottage, the pullover had shrunk inches and I had some difficulty getting out of it! It was now just the right size for Bijju, the milkman's 12-year-old son. But it continued to shrink at every wash, and it is now being worn by Teju, Bijju's younger brother, who is eight.

At the dark windy corner in the bazaar, one always found an old man bent over his charcoal fire, roasting peanuts. He was probably quite tall, but I never saw him standing up. One judged his height from his long, loose limbs. He was very thin, probably tubercular, and the high cheekbones added to the tautness of his tightly stretched skin.

His peanuts were always fresh, crisp and hot. They were popular with small boys who had a few coins to spend on their way to and from school.

No one seemed to know the old man's name. One just took his presence for granted. He was as fixed a landmark as the clock tower or the old cherry tree that grew crookedly from the hillside. He seemed less perishable than the tree, more dependable than the clock. He had no family, but in a way all the world was his family because he was in continuous contact with people. And yet he was a remote sort of being; always polite, even to children, but never familiar. He was seldom alone, but he must have been lonely.

Summer nights he rolled himself up in a thin blanket and slept on the ground beside the dying embers of his fire. During winter he waited until the last cinema show was over before retiring to the rickshaw coolies' shelter where there was protection from the freezing wind.

He died last summer.

That corner remained very empty, very dark, and every time I passed it, I was haunted by visions of the old peanut vendor, troubled by the questions I did not ask; and I wondered if he was really as indifferent to life as he appeared to be.

Then, a few weeks ago, there was a new occupant of the corner, a new seller of peanuts. No relative of the old man, but a boy of 13 or 14. The human personality can impose its own nature on its surroundings. In the old man's time it seemed a dark, gloomy corner. Now it's lit up by sunshine—a sunny personality, smiling, chattering. Old age gives way to youth; and I'm glad I won't be alive when the new peanut vendor grows old. One shouldn't see too many people grow old.

Leaving the main bazaar behind, I walk some way down the Mussoorie–Tehri road, a fine road to walk on, in spite of the dust from an occasional bus or jeep. From Mussoorie to Chamba, a distance of some 35 miles, the road seldom descends below 7,000 ft. and there is a continual vista of the snow range to the north and valleys and rivers to the south. Dhanaulti is one of the lovelier spots, and the Garhwal Mandal Vikas Nigam has a rest house here, where one can spend an idyllic weekend.

Leaving the Tehri Road, one can also trek down to the little Aglar river and then up to Nag Tibba, 9,000 ft., which has an oak forest and animals ranging from the barking-deer to the Himalayan bear; but this is an arduous trek and you must be prepared to spend the night in the open.

On this particular day I reach Suakholi, and rest in a teashop, a loose stone structure with a tin-roof held down by stones. It serves the bus passengers, mule drivers, milkmen and others who use this road.

I find a couple of mules tethered to a pine tree. The mule drivers, handsome men in tattered clothes, sit on a bench in the shade of the tree, drinking tea from brass tumblers. The shopkeeper, a man of indeterminate age—the cold dry winds from the mountain passes having crinkled his face like a walnut—greets me enthusiastically. He even produces a chair, which looks a survivor from one of Wilson's rest houses and may even be a Sheration. Fortunately, the Mussoorie *kabaris* do not know about it or they'd have snapped it up long ago. In any case the stuffing has come out of the seat. The shopkeeper apologises for its condition: "The rats were nesting in it." And then, to reassure me: "But they have gone now."

I would just as soon be on the bench with the Jaunpuri mule-drivers, but I do not wish to offend Mela Ram, the teashop owner; so I take his chair.

"How long have you kept this shop?"

"Oh, 10–15 years, I do not remember."

He hasn't bothered to count the years. Why should he, outside the towns in the isolation of the hills, life is simply a matter of yesterday, today and tomorrow.

Unlike Mela Ram, the mule drivers have somewhere to go and something to deliver: sacks of potatoes! From Jaunpur to Jaunsar, the potato is probably the crop best suited to these stony, terraced fields. They have to deliver their potatoes in Landour Bazaar and return to their village before nightfall; and soon they lead their pack animals away, along the dusty road to Mussoorie.

"Tea or lassi?" Mela Ram offers me a choice, and I choose the curd preparation, which is sharp and sour and very refreshing. The wind sighs gently in the upper branches of the pine trees, and I relax in my Sheration chair like some eighteenth-century nawab who has brought his own furniture into the wilderness.

Having wandered some way down the Tehri road, it is quite late by the time I return to the Landour Bazaar. Lights still twinkle on the hills, but shop fronts are shuttered and the little bazaar is silent. The people living on either side of the narrow street can hear my footsteps, and I hear their casual remarks, music, a burst of laughter.

Through a gap in the rows of buildings, I can see Pari Tibba outlined in the moonlight. A greenish phosphorescent glow appears to move here and there about the hillside. This is the "fairy light" that gives the hill its name Pari Tibba, Fairy Hill. I have no explanation for it, and I don't know anyone else who has been able to explain it satisfactorily; but often from my window I see this greenish light zigzagging about the hill.

A three-quarter moon is up, and the tin roofs of the bazaar, drenched with drew, glisten in the moonlight. Although the street is unlit, I need no torch. I can see every step of the way. I can even read the headlines on the discarded newspaper lying in the gutter.

Although I am alone on the road, I am aware of the life pulsating around me. It is a cold night, doors and windows are shut; but through the many chinks, narrow fingers of light reach out into the night. Who could still be up? A shopkeeper going through his accounts, a college student preparing for his exams, someone coughing and groaning in the dark.

A jackal slinks across the road, looking right and left he knows his road-drill to make sure the dogs have gone; A field rat wriggles through a hole in a rotting plank on its nightly foray among sacks of grain and pulses.

Yes, this is an old bazaar. The bakers, tailors, silversmith and wholesale merchants are the grandsons of those who followed the mad sahibs to this hilltop in the 30s and 40s of the last century. Most of them are plainsmen, quite prosperous even though many of their houses are crooked and shaky.

Although the shopkeepers and tradesmen are fairly prosperous, the hill people, those who come from the surrounding Tehri and Jaunpur villages, are usually poor. Their small holdings and rocky fields do not provide them with much of a living, and men and boys have often to come into the hill station or go down to the cities in search of a livelihood. They pull rickshaws or work in hotels and restaurants. Most of them have somewhere to stay.

But as I pass along the deserted street, under the shadow of the clock tower, I find a boy huddled in a recess, a thin shawl wrapped around his shoulders. He is wide awake and shivering.

I pass by, my head down, my thoughts already on the warmth of my small cottage only a mile away. And then I stop. It is almost as though the bright moonlight has stopped me, holding my shadow in thrall.

*'If I am not for myself,
who will be for me?
And, if I am not for others,
what am I?
And if not now, when?'*

The words of an ancient sage beat upon my mind. I walk back to the shadows where the boy crouches. He does not say anything, but he looks up at me, puzzled and apprehensive. All the warnings of well-wishers crowd in upon me—stories of crime by night, of assault and robber, "ill met by moonlight."

But this is not Northern Ireland or the Lebanon or the streets of New York. This is Landour in the Garhwal Himalayas. And the boy is no criminal. I can tell from his features that he comes from the hills beyond Tehri. He has come here looking for work and he has yet to find any.

"Have you somewhere to stay?" I asked.

He shakes his head; but something about my tone of voice has given him confidence, because there is a glimmer of hope, a friendly appeal in his eyes.

I have committed myself. I cannot pass on. A shelter for the night—that's the very least one human should be able to expect from another.

"If you can walk some way," I offer, "I can give you a bed and blanket."

He gets up immediately, a thin boy, wearing only a shirt and part of an old track-suit. He follows me without any hesitation. I cannot now betray his trust. Nor can I fail to trust him.

The Old Lama

I meet him on the road every morning, on my walk up to the Landour post office. He is a lean old man in a long maroon robe, a Tibetan monk of uncertain age. I'm told he's about 85. But age is really immaterial in the mountains. Some grow old at their mother's breasts, and there are others who do not age at all.

If you are like this old Lama, you go on forever. For he is a walking man, and there is no way you can stop him from walking.

Kim's Lama, rejuvenated by the mountain air, strode along with "steady, driving strokes," leaving his disciple far behind. My Lama, older and feebler than Kim's, walks very slowly, with the aid of an old walnut walking-stick. The ferrule keeps coming off the end of the stick, but he puts it back with coal-tar left behind by the road repairers.

The Old Lama

He plods and shuffles along. In fact, he is very like the tortoise in the story of the hare and the tortoise. I see him walking past my window, and five minutes later when I start out on the same road, I feel sure of overtaking him half way up the hill. But invariably I find him standing near the post-office when I get there.

He smiles when he sees me. We are always smiling at each other. His English is limited, and I have absolutely no Tibetan. He has a few words of Hindi, enough to make his needs known, but that is about all. He is quite happy to converse silently with all the creatures and people who take notice of him on the road.

It is the same walk he takes every morning. At nine o'clock, if I look out of my window, I can see a line of Tibetan prayer-flags fluttering over an old building in the cantonment. He emerges from beneath the flags and starts up the steep road. Ten minutes later he is below my window, and sometimes he stops to sit and rest on my steps, or on a parapet further along the road. Sooner or later, coming or going, I shall pass him on the road or up near the post-office. His eyes will twinkle behind thick-lensed glasses, and he will raise his walking-stick slightly in salutation. If I say something to him, he just smiles and nods vigorously in agreement.

An agreeable man. He was one of those who came to India in 1959, fleeing the Chinese occupation of Tibet. His Holiness the Dalai Lama found sanctuary in India, and lived in Mussoorie for a couple of years; many of his followers settled here. A new generation of Tibetans has grown up in the hill-station, and those under 30 years have never seen their homeland. But for almost all of them—and there are several thousand in this district alone— Tibet is their country, their real home, and they are quick to express their determination to go back when their land is free again.

Even a 20-year-old girl like Tseten, who has grown up knowing English and Hindi, speaks of the day when she will return to Tibet with her parents. She has given me a painting of Milarepa, the Buddhist monk-philosopher, meditating beneath a fruit-laden peach tree, the eternal snows in the background. This is, perhaps, her vision of the Tibet she would like to see, some day. Meanwhile, she works as a typist in the office of the Tibetan Homes Foundation.

My old Lama will, I am sure, be among the first to return, even if he has to walk all the way, over the mountain passes. Maybe, that's why he plods up and around this hill every day. He is practising for the long walk back to Tibet. Here he is again, pausing at the foot of my steps. It's a cool, breezy morning, and he does not feel the need to sit down.

"Tashi-tilay!" (Good day!) I greet him, in the only Tibetan I know.

"Tashi-tilay!" he responds, beaming with delight.

"Will you go back to Tibet one day?" I ask him for the first time.

In spite of his limited Hindi, he understands me immediately, and nods vigorously.

"Soon, soon!" he exclaims, and raises his walking stick to emphasise his words.

Yes, if the Tibetans are able to return to their country, he will be among the first to go back. His heart is still on that high plateau. And like the tortoise, he will be there waiting for the young hare to catch up with him.

If he goes, I shall certainly miss him on my walks.

Visitors from the Forest

When mist fills the Himalayan valleys, and heavy monsoon rain sweeps across the hills, it is natural for wild creatures to seek shelter. And sometimes my cottage in the forest is the most convenient refuge.

There is no doubt I make things easier for all concerned by leaving most of my windows open. I like plenty of fresh air indoors, and if a few birds, beasts and insects come in too, they're welcome, provided they don't make too much of a nuisance of themselves.

I must confess, I did lose patience with a bamboo beetle who blundered in the other night and fell into the water jug. I rescued him and pushed him out of the window. A few seconds later he came whirring in again, and with unerring accuracy landed with a plop in the same jug. I fished him out once more and offered him the freedom of the night. But attracted no doubt by the light and warmth of my small sitting-room, he came buzzing back, circling the room like a helicopter looking for a place to land. Quickly I covered the water jug. He landed in a bowl of wild dahlias, and I allowed him to remain there, comfortably curled up in the hollow of a flower.

Sometimes during the day a bird visits me—a deep blue whistling thrush, hopping about on long, dainty legs, too nervous to sing. She perches on the window-sill, looking out at the rain. She does not permit any familiarity. But if I sit quietly in my chair she will sit quietly on my window sill, glancing quickly at me now and then to make sure I am keeping my distance. When the rain stops, she glides away, and it is only then, confident in her freedom, that she bursts into full-throated song, her broken but haunting melody echoing down the ravine.

A squirrel comes sometimes, when his home in the oak tree gets water-logged. Apparently he is a bachelor; anyway, he lives alone. He knows me well, this squirrel, and is bold enough to climb on to the dining table looking for titbits which he always finds because I leave them there deliberately. Had I met him when he was a youngster, he would have learnt to eat from my hand; but I have only been here for a few months. I like it this way. I am not looking for pets; these are simply guests.

Last week, as I was sitting down at my desk to write a long-deferred article, I was startled to see an emerald-green praying mantis sitting on my writing-pad. He peered at me with his protuberant glass-bead eyes, and I stared down at him through my glasses. When I gave him a prod, he moved off in a leisurely way. Later, I found him examining the binding of *Leaves of Grass*; perhaps he had found a succulent bookworm. He disappeared for a couple of days, and then I found him on my dressing-table, preening himself before the mirror.

Out in the garden, I spotted another mantis, perched on the jasmine bush. Its arms were raised like a boxer's. Perhaps they are a pair, I thought, and went indoors, fetched my mantis and placed him on the jasmine bush opposite his fellow insect. He did not like what he saw—no comparison with his own image!—and made off in a hurry.

My most interesting visitor comes at night, when the lights are still burning—a tiny bat who prefers to fly in through the open door, and will use the window only if there is no alternative. His object is to snap up the moths who cluster round the lamps.

All the bats I have seen fly fairly high, keeping near the ceiling; but this particular bat flies in low like a dive bomber, zooming in and out of chair legs and under tables. Once he passed straight between my legs. Has his radar gone wrong, I wondered, or is he just plain mad?

I went to my shelves of natural history and looked up bats, but could find no explanation for this erratic behaviour. As a last resort I turned to an ancient volume, Sterndale's *Indian Mammalia* (Calcutta, 1884), and in it, to my delight, found what I was looking for: "A bat found near Mussoorie by Captain Hutton, on the southern range of hills at 1,800 metres; head and body about three centimetres, skims close to the ground, instead of flying high as bats generally do. Habitat, Jharipani, north-west Himalayas." Apparently, the bat was rare even in 1884.

Perhaps I have come across one of the few surviving members of the species. Jharipani is only three kilometres from where I live. I am happy that this bat survives in my small corner of the woods, and I undertake to celebrate it in prose and verse. Once, I found it suspended upside down from the railing at the foot of my bed. I decided to leave it there. For a writer alone in the woods, even an eccentric bat is welcome company.

Sanctuary Features

A Bouquet of Love

The Oaks, Hunter's Lodge, The Parsonage, The Pines, Dumbarnie, Mackinnon's Hall and Windamere—these are names of some of the old houses that still stand on the outskirts of our hill-stations. They were built over a hundred years ago by British settlers who sought relief from the searing heat of the plains. Most have fallen into decay and are now inhabited by wild cats, owls, goats, and the occasional mule-driver.

But among these neglected mansions stands a neat, white-washed cottage, Mulberry Lodge. And in it lived an elderly English spinster named Miss Mackenzie. She was well over eighty, but no one would have guessed it. She was sprightly and wore old-fashioned but well-preserved dresses. Once a week, she walked to town and bought butter, jam, soap and sometimes a bottle of eau-de-cologne.

Miss Mackenzie had lived there since her teens, before World War I. Her parents, brother and sister were dead. She had no relatives in India, and lived on a small pension and gift parcels sent from a childhood friend. She had few visitors—the local padre, the postman, the milkman. Like other lonely old people, she kept a pet, a large black cat with bright, yellow eyes.

In a small garden she grew dahlias, chrysanthemums, gladioli and a few rare orchids. She knew a great deal about wild flowers, trees, birds and insects. She never seriously studied them, but had an intimacy with all that grew and flourished around her.

It was September, and the rains were nearly over. Miss Mackenzie's African marigolds were blooming. She hoped the coming winter wouldn't be too severe because she found it increasingly difficult to bear the cold. One day, as she was pottering about in her garden, she saw a schoolboy plucking wild flowers on the slope above the cottage. "What're you up to, young man?" she called.

Alarmed, the boy tried to dash up the hillside, but slipped on pine needles and slid down the slope into Miss Mackenzie's nasturtium bed. Finding no escape he gave a bright smile and said, "Good morning, Miss."

He attended the local English medium school, and wore a blazer and a tie. Like most polite schoolboys, he called every woman 'Miss'.

"Good morning," said Miss Mackenzie severely. 'Would you mind moving out of my flower bed?"

The boy stepped gingerly over the nasturtiums and looked at Miss Mackenzie with appealing eyes.

"You ought to be in school," she said. "What're you doing here?"

"Picking flowers, Miss." He held up a bunch of ferns and wild flowers.

"Oh," Miss Mackenzie was disarmed. It had been a long time since she had seen a boy taking an interest in flowers.

"Do, you like flowers?" she asked.

"Yes, Miss. I'm going to be a botan ... a botanitist?"

"You mean a botanist?"

"Yes, Miss."

"That's unusual. Do you know the names of these flowers?"

"No, Miss."

"This is a buttercup," said Miss Mackenzie. "And that purple stuff is Salvia. Do you have any books on flowers?"

"No, Miss."

"Come in and I'll show you one."

She led the boy into a small front room crowded with furniture, books, vases and jam jars. He sat awkwardly on the edge of a chair. The cat jumped on to his knees and settled down, purring softly.

"What's your name?" asked Miss Mackenzie, as she rummaged through her books.

"Anil, Miss."

"And where do you live?"

"When school closes, I go to Delhi. My father has a business there."

"Oh, and what's that?"

"Bulbs, Miss."

"Flower bulbs?"

"No. Electric bulbs."

"Ah, here we are!" she said taking a heavy volume from the shelf. "*Flora Himaliensis*, published in 1892, and probably the only copy in India. This is a valuable book, Anil. No other naturalist has recorded as many wild Himalayan flowers. But there are still many plants unknown to the botanists who spend all their time at microscopes instead of in the mountains. Perhaps you'll do something about that one day."

"Yes, Miss."

She lit the stove, and put the kettle on for tea. And then the old English lady and the small Indian boy sat side by side, absorbed in the book. Miss Mackenzie pointed out many flowers that grew around the hill-station, while the boy made notes of their names and seasons.

"May I come again?" asked Anil, when finally he rose to go.

"If you like," said Miss Mackenzie. "But not during school hours. You mustn't miss your classes."

After that, Anil visited Miss Mackenzie about once a week, and nearly always brought a wild flower for her to identify. She looked forward to the boy's visits. Sometimes, when more than a week passed and he didn't come, she would grumble at the cat.

By the middle of October, with only a fortnight left before school closed, snow fell on the distant mountains.

One peak stood higher above the others, a white pinnacle against an azure sky. When the sun set, the peak turned from orange to pink to red.

"How high is that mountain?" asked Anil.

"It must be over 12,000 feet," said Miss Mackenzie. "I always wanted to go there, but there is no proper road. At the height, there'll be flowers that you don't get here—blue gentian, purple columbine."

The day before school closed, Anil came to say goodbye. As he was about to leave, Miss Mackenzie thrust the *Flora Himaliensis* into his hands.

"It's so valuable!" he said.

"That's why I'm giving it to you. Otherwise, it will fall into the hands of the junk dealers."

"But, Miss..."

"Don't argue."

The boy tucked the book under his arm, stood at attention, and said, "Good-bye, Miss Mackenzie." It was the first time he had spoken her name.

Strong winds soon brought rain and sleet, killing the flowers in the garden. The cat stayed indoors, curled up at the foot of the bed. Miss Mackenzie wrapped herself in old shawls and mufflers, but still felt cold. Her fingers grew so stiff that it took almost an hour to open a can of baked beans. Then it snowed, and for several days the milkman did not come.

Tired, she spent most of her time in bed. It was the warmest place. She kept a hot-water bottle against her back, and the cat kept her feet warm. She dreamed of spring and summer. In three months, the primroses would be out, and Anil would return.

One night the hot-water bottle burst, soaking the bed. The sun didn't shine for several days, and the blankets remained damp. Miss Mackenzie caught a chill and had to keep to her cold, uncomfortable bed.

A strong wind sprang up one night and blew the bedroom window open. Miss Mackenzie was too weak to get up and close it. The wind swept the rain and sleet into the room. The cat snuggled close to its mistress's body. Toward morning, the body lost its warmth, and the cat left the bed and started scratching about the floor.

As sunlight streamed through the window, the milkman arrived. He poured some milk into the saucer on the doorstep, and the cat jumped down from the window-sill.

The milkman called a greeting to Miss Mackenzie. There was no answer. Knowing she was always up before sunrise, he poked his head in the open window and called again.

Miss Mackenzie did not answer. She had gone to the mountain, where the blue gentian and purple columbine grow.